CARLY'S REVENGE

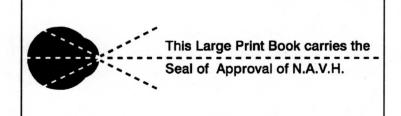

This Large Print Book carries the
Seal of Approval of N.A.V.H.

A CARLY BARTON NOVEL

CARLY'S REVENGE

DAVID OSBORNE

THORNDIKE PRESS
A part of Gale, Cengage Learning

GALE
CENGAGE Learning·

Farmington Hills, Mich • San Francisco • New York • Waterville, Maine
Meriden, Conn • Mason, Ohio • Chicago

GALE
CENGAGE Learning·

LIBRARY OF CONGRESS CATALOGING-IN-PUBLICATION DATA

Names: Osborne, David, 1943– author.
Title: Carly's revenge : a Carly Barton novel / by David Osborne.
Description: Large print edition. | Waterville, Maine : Thorndike Press, a part of Gale, Cengage Learning, 2017. | Series: Thorndike Press large print western
Identifiers: LCCN 2017007711| ISBN 9781432839284 (hardcover) | ISBN 1432839284 (hardcover)
Subjects: LCSH: Large type books. | BISAC: FICTION / Historical. | FICTION / Westerns. | GSAFD: Western stories.
Classification: LCC PS3615.S273 C37 2017 | DDC 813/.6—dc23
LC record available at https://lccn.loc.gov/2017007711

Published in 2017 by arrangement with David Osborne

Printed in the United States of America
1 2 3 4 5 6 7 21 20 19 18 17

To my brothers and sisters
who had the imagination to play cowboys
and Indians with me and even allow me
to win occasionally.

ACKNOWLEDGMENTS

To my wife, Pat, and family who generously gave of their time to read and provide insight for this book.

CHAPTER 1

The sun's position overhead told Carly Barton it was late afternoon. She was finishing her chores in the barn after milking the family cow. She had fed the cow but she still had to feed the three horses, the chickens, and gather the eggs. The sound of horses coming in temporarily interrupted her thoughts and her work.

At first she ignored the riders but, out of curiosity, she stepped to the door of the barn and looked out. She watched for a few moments as three men rode into the yard and dismounted in front of the house. Her father came out of the house and spoke to the men. She could not hear the conversation so turned back to her work.

Carly and her family had moved here on the Kansas plains only a few months ago and they'd had few visitors. Some were just riding through, others were looking for a job, and still others hoping for a handout.

9

Her father was not very generous, but her mother would never leave anyone out in the cold without at least giving them food and water. This was probably another chance for her to feed someone.

It took several minutes to finish her chores. Finally, she left the barn, closed the door, and headed for the house carrying the full milk bucket and a basket of eggs. When she got close to the house, she stopped when she saw the three horses hitched to the rail. They stood slipshod, lathered up, and heads drooping. It did not take an expert to figure out the horses had been ridden hard. They had no water, even though the trough was a mere four feet away. Carly's anger flared. Cruelty to animals, especially horses, was unforgivable in her book.

She did not see the riders anywhere around, so she assumed they were inside the house with her parents. She reached the porch, and as she started to climb the steps, she heard two gunshots and her mother screaming. She dropped the egg basket and milk bucket and ran up the steps to the door. She no longer cared about eggs or milk. Before she could open the door, there were two more gunshots, and the screaming stopped.

She pushed the door open, rushed inside, stopped, and stared at the ghastly scene. Her mother lay on the kitchen floor with her green gingham dress soaked in a pool of blood. Off to her left was her father. He sat in a straight back kitchen chair with his hands tied behind his back. His head lay on his chest and Carly could see a bullet hole in his forehead and another in his chest. Blood slowly oozed from both wounds. She screamed, ran to her mother, and dropped to her knees at her mother's side. She was crying, yelling, and wracked by grief and the beginning of a terrible rage. Tears flowed down her cheeks as she bent down and wiped the blood from her mother's face with her hand. Two strong hands grabbed her from behind, roughly jerked her to her feet, and held her in a tight embrace.

Carly had paid no attention to the three men when she opened the door and ran inside. She could not see the man who held her now, but she could see the other two. The one nearest to her was a large man with a scraggly red beard and a protruding stomach. He carried a gun stuck in the belt of his trousers on one side and a large knife in a sheath on his other side. Standing farther away was a young man who might be handsome except his nose was crooked

11

and it was much too big for his face. There were scars on his neck, much like rope burns. He stood off to the side, face turned away from all of them, gazing off in space, his jaw set, clenching his teeth.

"Well, well, now, what do we have here?" asked the big man with the beard. He moved closer so he was only a foot from her and grabbed her shoulder hard.

"Let me go," Carly shouted, trying to break loose from the man's grasp.

"Jist stop your fightin' an' relax," the man holding her said as he squeezed harder.

"Who are you and what did you do?" she asked through her tears.

"It don't matter who we are, and nothin' bad will happen to you if you behave yourself," the big man replied with an ugly grin.

"I'm sure she'll enjoy our company," said the man behind her, laughing.

She ignored his comment, "Why did you kill my mom and dad?" she cried, still trying to jerk away from the man holding her.

"Just stand still. I'll ask all the questions, missy, and, if you behave, you may not end up dead like these two," replied the bearded man as he pointed his index finger toward the dead couple.

"Why'd you kill them? They didn't do anything to you," she hollered.

"We need food, money, and whiskey, and we didn't get the right answers. They weren't cooperative, you see, so this should be a lesson for you." The man sneered.

"My mother would have fed you, and there's no money in the house anyway," she wailed.

"That old woman wouldn't be quiet. As for the money and whiskey, I'll be the judge of that. We'll search every inch of this place till we find what we want," he replied.

Carly still struggled to free herself, but to no avail. The man holding her tightened his grip and snickered. "What ya want me to do with her boss?"

"Just hold her still and let me look at her real good. She's a fine-looking woman."

"Wes, you're enjoying yourself too much. You've been in jail too long," Rod Ulrich said.

"You're damn right. Five years in that hellhole called Kansas State Prison. I ain't even seen one woman that whole time, never mind being close enough to touch one," replied Wes Stone.

"Well, you can touch this one. She ain't gonna mind. She ain't just any ordinary woman, she's beautiful," the man holding her said.

"Can't disagree with that," the big man

answered with a huge smile.

Carly tried to get away again, when the man loosened his grip, but he just squeezed her harder. "You're hurting me," she yelled.

The man named Stone reached out, grabbed one of Carly's breasts, squeezed hard, and she screamed again. "Maybe I've been in prison, but maybe I'm gonna make up for lost time," he said with an ugly grin.

Carly yelled and kicked out with her right foot. The big man quickly let loose of her breast and stepped back, avoiding her wicked kick.

"Keep your hands off me, you . . . you . . . you animal," she bellowed as tears streamed down her face.

"Ah . . . I love my women with spirit, and this one's a hellcat," said the big man in a booming voice.

"I'm not your woman, and I'll kill you the first chance I get," snapped Carly as she blinked and shook her head to clear the tears from her eyes.

The big man reached down, slipped out his big knife, and put it up to her throat. "Now missy, you ain't gonna kill no one, and me and you are gonna reach an understandin'. You'll be nice to me as long as I need you, or as long as I tell you, you understan'?"

Carly stopped squirming but did not respond. The big man removed the knife long enough to slap her face hard and then pushed the point of the knife blade back to her throat so hard that blood trickled from the puncture wound. Blood from her nose, mixed with tears, ran into her mouth, down her chin, and dropped onto her blouse. She choked and coughed, but was so stunned she did not raise her head.

The man pulled the knife back from her throat and spoke calmly. "Now missy, when I ask you a question, you'll answer me, and you'll answer me quick, and keep a civil tongue in your mouth. You understan'?"

She did not respond immediately and the big man drew back his fist. She was stubborn, but she decided the man could, and probably would, kill her with his fist or his knife. "Yes," she muttered.

"Now you're gettin' smart, missy."

The big man looked over at the younger man, "Kirby, drag these bodies outta here before they start stinkin' the place up."

"Stone, let's just leave 'em be and ride out. Those prison guards could be here any time now, or lawmen from all over the territory," said the youngest of the three men.

"Those guards probably quit a long time ago, and where else could we go with dark

15

coming on anyway?" Stone responded.

"You know damn well the law isn't going to stop chasing us. After you killed that guard, and you didn't have to do that, they'll never stop. Then you ambushed and killed those two other men on the way here. They're going to chase us all the way to hell, and it's your fault," snapped the young man.

"Look, you fool, we needed clothing, food, and guns. Besides, their horses was much better 'an ours."

The man holding Carly nodded his head and said, "Stone is right, you know. These clothes fit me just right an' my horse was no good."

"Shut up, Rod. You have no brains at all. You'd agree with him if he told you to go to hell," said Kirby.

"You can't talk to me like that," Rod yelled at him.

"Both of you, shut up. If we leave now, we got dead tired horses on the trail and nothin' to eat. Here we got a house with plenty of food, water, and probably some money and whiskey 'round somewheres. No, we can ride out tomorrow, and we'll be in Rock Springs in a few days. Now do what I told you to do and git rid of them bodies," he said sternly.

"Stone, you killed that prison guard and

those men on purpose. They're never going to stop chasing us. Besides, I didn't help you break out of prison so that I could be your damn slave," snarled Kirby.

"I killed that guard 'cause he pushed me too hard. He thought 'cause he was a guard, I had to do anything he told me to do. Well, I shore as hell showed him."

"Yes, you sure showed him, and now look what a fix we're in. Now you're trying to push me and I don't like it," replied Kirby angrily. He squared himself and dropped his hand down to the gun he had taken off another prison guard during the escape.

Wes Stone knew that Kirby Wilson was fast with a gun, but he did not think the young man would pull the weapon on him here and now, so he took three quick steps and backhanded the young man. The lick with Stone's huge paw sent Kirby sprawling across the floor. Stone pulled the gun from his britches. "Now, do what I told you, before I get mad," he roared.

Kirby put his hand to his face and found his nose bleeding from the punch. He wiped it off with the sleeve of his shirt and slowly stood up. He backed away a couple of steps and looked at the big man. He measured his chances with Stone's gun already pointing at him and decided that the odds were not in his favor. He turned toward the dead man.

"There'll be another time, Stone," he snapped.

Rod, still holding Carly, interrupted the argument. "Stone, you forgot 'bout the girl. We can use her. If the guards or lawmen show up, we got us a bargaining chip."

"Rod, I think you jist might be on to something." Stone slid the gun back in his britches and then looked over at Kirby. "I might even share her with you, if you do as I say." Stone thought by throwing Kirby a little bit, it might keep him in line better.

"I don't want nothin' to do with you nor that woman," the young man snarled.

"Can't you help me, please?" Carly said as she looked over at Kirby. "I'm begging you."

The big man ignored her plea to Kirby, but slid the knife from its sheath again and this time pointed it at Kirby, "Boy, don't give me no sass. I don't give a damn if you want her or not, and I don't give a damn whether you like me, but you'll do what I tell you, or I'll skin you alive. Now, when we get outta this territory you can go your own way but, until then, I'm the boss around here."

Kirby gazed at the big man with hate-filled

eyes, muttered under his breath, but did what Stone told him to do. He took out his knife, cut the ropes holding the dead man, and the limp body of Carly's father hit the floor hard.

"Leave him alone. I'll take care of him myself," Carly yelled at Kirby.

Kirby hesitated a moment, looking directly at Carly for the first time, then looked back down at the dead man.

"He's dead. It won't hurt him none. Go on an' git him outside. You can do whatever you want with 'em tomorrow," said Stone, looking directly at Carly. "If you're still alive."

Kirby took Carly's father's legs, dragging him through the door and onto the porch with Carly still screaming for him to leave her father alone.

"All right, Rod, turn her loose. She's gonna fix us some grub."

"What if she tries to make a run for it?" asked Rod, still holding onto her.

Stone looked at Carly and shook the knife at her close up. "If you try and run, I'll shoot you and carve you into tiny pieces. You got that?"

Carly nodded. When Rod released her, she rubbed her hands and arms, trying to get the blood circulating again. Kirby came back inside and started dragging Carly's mother outside. Carly screamed again and started toward him, but all that got her was Stone's fist in her stomach. She doubled over, thinking that she was going to vomit, but she had no chance. The big man put his boot against her bottom and pushed hard. Carly went down on one knee and almost fell to the floor from his push, but caught herself on the corner of the table and held on.

"Git over to that stove and start cookin' some grub. I'm gonna be watching you every minute."

After a few moments, she struggled to her feet.

"Don't hurt her, Stone. I want her to be healthy 'nough for some fun later," said Rod gleefully.

"I'm not gonna hurt the good parts. Besides, she'll be good enough for you when I get finished, won't you, missy?" he replied mockingly as he reached out and pushed her again.

Carly, still in pain and dizzy from the big man's fist, stumbled, and again almost fell to the floor. Her determination to put distance between her and the big man kept her on her feet. If she were busy, they would not hit her. She headed to the stove, trying not to step in her mother's blood covering a large part of the floor.

In spite of the pain in her stomach, she picked up some wood and slipped it in the stove to build up the fire. She pushed the coffee pot to the back of the stove. She was having difficulty thinking but knew she wanted these men gone. Within a few minutes, she had some flapjacks cooking in a skillet. She sliced off some bacon and dropped it in another skillet, then slid the coffee pot over to the hottest part of the stove.

The three men were now sitting at the kitchen table. "Hurry up with that grub," the big man yelled.

"How about that whiskey?" asked Rod.

"Yes, missy, I know you got some whiskey stashed around here somewhere, you may as well tell where it's at," said Stone.

"I don't drink and I don't know anything about any whiskey," snapped Carly, keeping her eyes on the stove.

"Woman, you keep a civil tongue in your mouth if you know what's good for you. Rod, you search the whole house. See if you can find any money, whiskey, or anything else we can use," demanded Stone.

"Okay, boss, I'm sure I can find some good stuff around here somewhere," replied

Rod gleefully as he stood and moved away from the table.

Carly knew that her father kept whiskey around the house, usually for medicinal purposes, but she was hoping they would not be able to find it. She was afraid things would be even worse for her if the men were drunk, so she was not going to help in any way. She knew there were a few dollars in the house and she was certainly not going to help them find that. She would need money, if she could survive. Then for a second she was very afraid, knowing their intent was to kill her, just like her parents. Fear turned to hatred, and suddenly all she wanted to do was to kill them.

The convict searched the entire house and he came up with two bottles of whiskey. One was full, but the other was open, and only half-full. Stone took the full bottle and told Rod and Kirby they could share the other. Kirby refused to drink, so Rod was glad to drink the rest of the bottle by himself.

"Didn't see no money nowhere," said Rod.

"We'll try again before we leave, and we'll have this purty young lady to help us find it," replied Wes Stone.

Carly ignored them and waited as long as she dared to serve the food. She even allowed the flapjacks and bacon to burn before she served them. She knew she was running a risk, but she got some satisfaction from making them wait. She needed time, and her mind was not working well. It was not long before they started hollering for coffee, and then she finally dished out the food. When they started to eat, she said she needed to get some water and take care of the animals, but Stone insisted she sit down at the table with them.

He told her that someone would escort her when she went out. She refused to eat, but she did pour some coffee for herself, and sipped it while watching the men very carefully as they ate. She was beginning to think more clearly, but options appeared slim. She knew she was in trouble unless the prison people who were following the men showed up soon. She thought about neighbors, but the nearest ranch was the Johnson place, and it was more than five miles away. It was ten miles to town, and she knew that no one from town would be just dropping by. She needed to find some way to escape, but the men were watching her too closely. Even if she could escape, she was not sure she could reach the Johnson place with them trailing her. The three men ate all of the food she put on the table, not paying any attention to how burned it was. As they finished eating, she quickly picked up the dishes and carried them to the counter.

"Rod, you and Kirby go take care of the horses. Put 'em in the barn and make sure they get 'nough water and feed. See if the farmer's horses are any better'n ours are. We have a long way to travel tomorrow," said Stone.

Kirby stared hard at Stone. "Why do I have to do all the work?"

"We've been all through that boy, so git moving. I'm tired of your whining." Stone sneered.

Kirby stood up straight and looked at the big man. "You call me boy again and I will blow a hole in that big fat gut of yours."

Rod got up quickly and laid a hand on Kirby's shoulder. "Come on. Let's get the horses put up." As Kirby shook his hand off, Rod let go of him and headed for the door, but Kirby muttered under his breath as he stared at Stone. Finally, he turned and followed Rod outside.

"I have to bury my parents," said Carly, without any emotion.

Stone got up from the table, walked over to Carly, and put his hands on her shoulders. She managed not to flinch and did

24

not look at him. "You'll have plenty of time for that later. That is, if you play along with us and make sure that we have a good time tonight," said the big man with a devious grin.

"You should all leave now. There's another ranch just down the road. Somebody could be coming anytime now," she said without much conviction.

"Lady, we rode all around this place before we came in, and the nearest ranch is miles away so don't try and fool me. Besides, they'd be dead before they could get off their horses. And if you're plannin' to escape, it won't work. You'll be dead before you get a hundred yards from the house."

"Why don't you just kill me now and get it over with?" she replied sarcastically.

"Aw, you'd love that, wouldn't you? Well now, that would just spoil all the fun we're gonna have, so you just go ahead and git all riled up and we'll all enjoy it."

"I'm not going to enjoy anything from you, and I promise that I'm going to kill you as soon as I get a chance."

"I'm not worried much about that," he replied with an ugly laugh.

Carly moved away from the big man to remove more dishes from the table, but he continued to follow her everywhere she went. He would reach out to touch her and she would involuntarily flinch, as she tried to continue her work. Her mind was working now. She knew her father kept a rifle in the barn to shoot rats, and oh, how she would love to shoot this rat. They probably would not think to look for anything in the barn. If she could only get to it . . . But she was sure they would not let her go near the barn by herself. Stone finally sat down, never taking his eyes off her.

Carly picked up a pan to take to the counter where she had left the knife after slicing the bacon. If she could get the knife and hide it in her clothing, it might help her escape. She turned, edged closer to the counter, and reached behind her for the knife. Keeping her hand behind her and out of sight, she was able to get a hold on it. Just as she picked up the knife, the other two men came back into the house. She knew that with the three of them in the room, the knife would not do her much good, but she was not going to let go of it anyway. It might be her only chance.

CHAPTER 2

When the two men came inside the door after taking care of the horses, Kirby walked over to the stove, poured some coffee, and sat down at the table, staring at the outside door. Rod walked over to Stone. "Let's get on with the fun. I haven't had a woman in a long time."

"We got plenty of time, and you can't have her till after I'm done anyway," he answered.

"Okay, but I don't think I can wait," Rod responded.

"You can wait, but I'm gonna start now." Stone took another pull from the whiskey bottle and looked at Carly. "Get in the bedroom and get undressed."

"Let her undress in here. I want to see her naked," replied Rod.

"To hell with both of you. I'm not doing anything for any of you," Carly snapped back at them.

She was too close to the big man's fist,

which caught her in the jaw and knocked her against the counter. Her head rocked, and she almost dropped the knife. Until she was able to gain a steady footing, she held onto the counter while her head cleared.

"Now, you want some more of that?" Stone growled.

She was outraged, angry, and sore from his blows, but she knew getting beat up would not help her. She moved away from the counter and staggered to her parent's bedroom. She hoped that if one man came in by himself she could stab him with the knife and get through the window.

She walked inside the bedroom and waited for the hated man to come in. She thought how unfortunate it was that there were no locks on the doors, but she knew he would just break the door down anyway. Soon Stone came in and closed the door. He looked at her and pulled his knife. "Get undressed quick," he yelled, waving the knife in her face.

She stood with both hands behind her back and looked at him calmly, "You need to get rid of the gun and knife. You don't need those."

He smirked and stared at her. "No, I don't need 'em, but I'm keepin' 'em anyway. Now get undressed," he commanded.

She kept her left hand with the knife behind her back and started slowly unbuttoning her clothing with the right. She had to wait until he was close enough, but had learned not to let him get too close. She unbuttoned two buttons and stopped.

"I know we got all night, but you're taking too much time. Now git undressed, unless you want me to use this knife."

She unbuttoned another button and stopped again.

"I said get undressed," he barked and took a step to reach and grab her arm. When he was close enough, she swung the knife at the big man's stomach as hard as she could. He saw the knife and grabbed her hand just as the knife hit his stomach. The knife drew some blood, but he twisted her arm violently until she dropped the knife, then he smacked her so hard that she fell on the bed. She was not able to get up because he was on top of her, pulling and ripping at her clothing.

She struggled to get away but he was much too big and strong. She cried and screamed until he hit her again, and her last words to Stone were, "I'm going to kill all you bastards!"

There was a knock on the door and Rod

called out, "What're you trying to do, kill her?"

"Okay Ulrich, git away from that door. I'll let you know when I'm done."

She held on to her clothes as he pulled and yanked on them. Finally, he smacked her in the face. "You may as well give up or it's gonna be much worse," and he smacked her again.

She was weakening, and the pain from his blows was unbearable. She finally decided that whatever was going to happen, would happen anyway, and she could not stop him. She removed her hands from her clothing and let them drop to her side. Stone finished ripping off her clothes, leaving only a few tattered strips, and started groping her. At first, he tried to kiss her but she resisted. He quickly gave up on kissing, groped her body with both hands, and then raped her. He raped her repeatedly while she cried and struggled to get away. She was barely aware when Stone left the room. She curled up on the bed, hurt and weak, but unfortunately, her time alone did not last long.

She felt hands on her again and she knew that those hands belonged to the man named Rod Ulrich. She held her arms around her body, trying to keep him from raping her, but he jerked them away, slapped her hard a few times, and raped her. When she cried out, he started beating her again. At some point, she lost consciousness and, fortunately, did not remember anything more after that.

Kirby Wilson, the youngest of the three, had left the house and walked out to the barn for a smoke rather than listen to the screams of the woman. He did not approve of what his companions were doing, but he did not have enough nerve to try and stop them. He had looked into her eyes, pleading for help, and saw her expression turn to hatred. He knew that she was going to blame him right along with the others.

Long after the screams finally stopped, he walked back inside the house. The other two convicts had finally gone to sleep. They had dropped off in a drunken stupor after drinking the two bottles of whiskey. Kirby took a chair and rested his head on the kitchen table. He finally fell asleep but did not sleep well. In his dreams, he kept hearing men shouting and a woman screaming.

He finally gave up, got up, walked outside for another smoke, and found the sun was already on the horizon. After finishing the cigarette, he walked back inside, stoked up the fire, and put the coffee pot on. When it was boiling, he woke the other two men.

Rod wanted to get the woman up to fix them some breakfast, but Kirby demanded they leave her alone and get on the road. After a heated discussion, Kirby agreed to fix breakfast so they could leave. While he was cooking breakfast, the other two men went out to feed and water the horses. After they hurriedly ate their fill, they gathered up as much food as they could carry and put it in cloth sacks. When they finished, they went outside and hung the sacks on their saddles.

"Come on. We're ready to ride," said Kirby.

"Wait. I say we carry the bodies inside the house and burn it to the ground," said Rod.

"That might be a good idea. Nobody'll know we been here," agreed Stone.

"You're both crazy," snapped Kirby. "Fire and smoke will be seen for miles. The grass is so dry it could burn for miles around. We need to move out quickly and ride fast."

"We don't give a damn about the house or the grass. Besides, who's going to be seeing the smoke anyway?" asked Rod.

"There aren't many people around here, but Kirby's right. If the prison guards or lawmen are nearby they would see the smoke," replied Stone.

"So what're we going to do?" asked Rod.

Stone hesitated for a moment and looked around. "We do need to git rid of those bodies in case anyone rides up. Let's carry them behind the barn and cover 'em up."

"Why do we care?" snapped Kirby "We need to be far away fast."

"Damn it, Kirby, men riding by most likely won't go inside a house when no one's home. Now git going, and move those bodies like I said," replied Stone.

Kirby cursed under his breath but said nothing. He decided the sooner they got finished, the sooner they would be out of there.

Rod and Kirby picked up the man while Stone picked up the woman, and they carried the bodies behind the barn. They laid them close to the barn, covered them up with hay and straw, and then walked back to the front of the house. When they reached the porch, they noticed the blood on the floor.

"If anyone rides up they will see the blood on the porch," said Rod. "Burning the house down will git rid of the blood," he added.

"I'm runnin' this show," snapped Stone, "and I say we're not burning the house. Get a bucket and pump some water from that well. We'll get rid of the blood. It'll dry before anyone sees it."

"What about the woman?" asked Rod. "She for sure will tell about us."

"I've thought about the woman. We could take her with us," replied Stone.

"She's in no shape to ride," said Kirby. "In fact she might already be dead."

"How would you know?" asked Rod.

"I went to check on her," lied Kirby. "We just need to get as far from this place as possible."

"If you're all so afraid, I'll take care of her," Rod blurted out, an ugly grin on his face.

"Ulrich, you bastard, you probably took care of her already. You'd kill your own grandmother if it suited your fancy, but you're not going to kill that woman," snarled Kirby.

"And just who's going to stop me?"

Kirby faced Ulrich and adjusted his gun belt, "I will. You take one step toward that house and I'll shoot you."

Rod Ulrich was a fair hand with a gun, but from what he had heard, Kirby was much better. He glanced over at Wes Stone, but the big man said nothing. Since he was not going to get any backing from Stone, he began to back away.

"Well, guess we should just ride out," he

muttered.

Kirby turned his back to the man and walked over to get some water. After they washed the bloodstains, he threw down the bucket and stood next to his horse, waiting for the others to get ready.

"Git mounted and let's git out of here," growled Stone.

The other two men mounted, and they headed off in the direction of Rock Springs. Kirby Wilson was the last one to mount. He was the only one who looked back. He asked himself, why was he still riding with two men that he despised?

CHAPTER 3

Carly tried to open her swollen and battered eyes but it was too painful. She left them closed and lay still for some time, recalling what had happened. She remembered her parents' bodies and started to cry, then got extremely angry and the tears stopped. She must be alone, so she finally forced herself to open her eyes. She could not see anything. She tried to focus above the bed but everything was just a blur. She looked up farther, but could not even see the ceiling. Was it just too dark, or was she blinded from the beatings she took? She tried to raise her arm to rub her eyes with her hand but it hurt too much and she fell back to sleep, exhausted.

The next time she woke, she forced herself to look around, but the throbbing pain in her head and neck was too much for her to bear. She thought she heard loud voices. Were the men still in the house? Were those real people or were the noises merely the rattling in her head? In any case, if they were people, she could not hear what they were saying. Maybe they were not in the house. The pain and anger worsened as she remembered the three men and she knew she was hearing their voices. They seemed to be far away. She could not get up anyway. Her eyelids fluttered and she drifted off again.

Carly did not know how long she was out this time but hers was not restful sleep. She tossed and turned, her pain-wracked body keeping her from lying in any position very long. Finally, she woke and realized she was in her parents' large bed. Then, again, she remembered the awful ordeal. Was that yesterday? The bodies of her parents were still out on the porch. She had to do something. She could not just leave them on the porch.

She tried to move, but every bone in her body ached from the beatings she had endured. She remembered hearing voices earlier, and she strained to hear any type of noise. She heard nothing. She lifted her head, and the pain in her head and nausea in her stomach hit at the same time. Without warning vomit spewed from her mouth and onto the bed where her head had lain a few moments ago. She needed to move, or lay her head back down in the vomit. It took all of the strength she could muster to roll herself off the bed and onto the floor. When she landed on the floor, pain engulfed her, and she lost consciousness again.

When she next woke, she could feel the warm sunlight coming through the window and shining on her face. She remembered the voices.

Was that last night, or was it this morning, or days ago? She thought she remembered daylight through the window at the same time she heard the voices, but in her confused state, nothing made much sense. The three men must have left early in the morning. Now with the sun shining through the window, she had no idea what time it was or even what day it was.

Again, the memories of that night came flooding into her mind. Did all of that really happen, or was her mind playing tricks on her? She shook her head to try to clear her thoughts, but that only made her headache worse. Then she thought about her parents and remembered that they were dead, lying on the porch. A low moo came from the barn and she remembered the animals. There was no one to feed them or milk the cow.

In spite of her pain, she managed to rise

to her hands and knees. She put her hands on the bed and tried to pull herself up to her feet, without success. She tried again, and when the second try was unsuccessful, she crawled a little way and finally dragged herself out of the bedroom and down the short hall to the kitchen. She attempted to get into a chair, but her strength was gone. She reached up, grabbed the tablecloth, and pulled it toward her. The water bucket came along with the tablecloth to the edge of the table. She needed water and managed enough strength to sit against the table leg so she could reach the bucket handle. Tilting the bucket forward allowed her to reach the dipper. With shaking hands, she filled the dipper, brought it to her lips, and took a long drink. She flinched when the dipper touched her lips so she lifted her hand and felt her lips. They were split, bruised, and swollen, and there was dried blood on her fingers.

In spite of the pain, she put the dipper back up to her lips and drank the rest of the water, then let the dipper fall. After a few minutes, with difficulty, she reached the bucket handle and pulled it down. The water poured on her head, ran down her face, and over the little bit of what was left of her torn and tattered clothing. She needed to find something to wear. Lifting her arms was painful, but she managed to raise her right arm and wipe the water and blood from her face.

She leaned back against the chair, closed her eyes, and rested. A noise startled her, and she opened her eyes. The noise came again, and she realized one of the horses in the barn was kicking the stall and the cow was bawling. She was not sure how, but she must get to the barn to feed the animals. She thought she was feeling better, determination set in, and she used the chair to help her to her feet. She took one small step toward the front door, but she could not manage another, so she sat down on the chair. She rested for a while, hoping to regain her strength, but soon dozed off, with her head on the table.

She had no idea how long she had dozed this time but, when she woke, the sun was going down. It must be after five o'clock, and she must have slept most of the day. With some difficulty, she was able to get to her feet and stagger across the room. She pulled open the door and looked out. She did not see anyone, and the only sounds she heard were coming from the barn. Her head felt as though it would burst, so she leaned her head against the doorframe and closed her eyes. After a few moments, she opened her eyes as she remembered the bodies of her parents. She knew the man named Kirby Wilson had dragged them out on the porch, but they were not there now. There was a bucket and signs that someone had tried to wash away the blood. Her mind raced. Did the murderers bury her parents? Where? No. After what happened last night she was certain those awful men would not take time to dig a grave and bury two people.

What was she going to do now? She had to find the bodies and give them a proper burial. She needed to take care of the animals. How? Then what?

Carly was almost twenty-one and had never lived anywhere other than with her parents. They had moved from Ohio to Missouri, and then caught a wagon train headed to California. Her mother was not well, and she hated the traveling. When they reached Kansas, her father scouted around, found this land, and decided to leave the wagon train and start this farm. There was plenty of good ground and water, an ideal place for a farm with a few cows. *Stop daydreaming,* she told herself, *and do something.*

She staggered out the door and onto the porch. She looked around but there was no sign of the bodies. She knew she must find and bury them, but that would have to wait, because her body would not let her leave the porch. The two steps to the hitching post looked a mile away.

She managed to get back inside and sat down at the kitchen table. Her mind worked, as she tried to think where the villains had hidden the bodies of her parents. She rested for a few minutes, then stood and staggered to a small mirror on the wall. Carly did not recognize the face staring back at her from the mirror. Cuts, scratches, and bruises covered her face. Both of her eyes were black, and there was a large bump on her cheekbone. Her dress was in tatters as were her undergarments, and her body was covered with bruises and more blood. As she looked at herself in the mirror, she saw the faces of the men that had beaten and raped her. Now she knew what she was going to do.

Carly tore off her remaining ragged clothing and then wobbled, naked, down the hallway, using the wall to keep her steady. She went back into her parents' bedroom. She had dresses in her room but she did not intend to wear a dress, ever again. The closet was in disarray as well as the room. She looked until she found a pair of her father's pants and a shirt. She carried them to her room, which was a mess too, and laid them on the bed. She got a towel, wrapped it around her, and walked back to the kitchen. She picked up the water bucket and a bar of soap, and slowly walked outside to the water pump. She pumped the water, stopping to rest several times, until she filled the bucket. Too weak to walk back to the house, she painfully began splashing water on her body, lathered up, and rinsed off the soap. When she was satisfied she was as clean as she could get, she toweled herself off, wrapped the towel around her, and walked back inside the house. She went to her room, picked out some of her under-clothes, and struggled to slip them on.

She examined her father's trousers, found her sewing box, and altered the pants. She hurried through the task. The animals' protests were louder now, and bothered her. She tried on the pants and decided they were workable for now. She was not very good at sewing, even though her mother had tried hard to teach her. Sewing was not something she liked to do, so she guessed that might be the reason her sewing never looked right. She slipped on her father's long-sleeved shirt, stuffed the shirttails into the trousers, walked back over to the mirror, and looked at herself. Even though the clothes were too big, she looked somewhat better than the last time she looked in the mirror, except for her battered face. Regardless of how she looked, her condition would have to do. It had taken at least an hour to accomplish all of that, and now it was almost dark. The pain had not lessened but her determination was stronger.

She needed to eat something, but she knew the animals needed attention more than she did. Even though her body ached with every step, she walked out the door and down to the barn. She spent over an hour in the barn, taking care of the animals. She did not bother to find a bucket to milk the cow, but let the milk puddle on the ground. The darkness and her pain made everything take much longer than usual. She stopped a few times to rest and finally she finished. There were only three horses on the farm so Carly saddled her favorite, a gray mare named Brandy. Her mother's favorite too. She found the rifle her father had kept in the barn and slipped it in the scabbard. She looked around once more, led the mare up to the hitching rail in front of the house, and walked inside.

She searched for something to eat but found very little. Those men had ransacked the place and taken whatever they wanted. She did find some flour and salt. She had brought eggs with her from the barn so she fried them, made some gravy and two flat biscuits, then forced herself to eat a little. She gathered up the small amount of food the men had left and put it in a bag. When she was finished, she went to her bedroom and lay on the bed, hoping to get some sleep. She finally gave up and got out of bed. She saw that the sun had set and it was getting dark. Even though she only had a short time before nightfall, she had work to do. Earlier she had decided to leave right away. Now she asked herself if she should stay the night and leave tomorrow, or leave now. She decided she did not want to stay another night here in this house by herself.

She carried everything out to the horse, filled the saddlebags, and tied the last bag on. She began the search for her parents. She searched around the house, in the barn, and finally found the bodies hidden behind the barn. She decided to bury them a few feet from where she found them. She found a shovel and began digging. In spite of the lateness of the day, it was hot. Before she was finished, she got so sick that she vomited again and lay on the grass for a while until she could get back on her feet. She buried her parents together in a shallow grave and made a vow that she would return later to give them a proper burial.

She was ready to leave, but she had no money. She knew her mother had a mason jar with a little bit in it. If those convicts had not found it, she would use that money. She went back to the house, lit a lamp, and walked to her parents' bedroom. She moved the small table in the corner, bent down, lifted a loose board, and pulled out the jar. She counted out nine dollars and thirty-eight cents. She stuck the money in her pants pocket and went back to her room. She had managed to save a few dollars and kept it in a small bag under her dresser. She got down on her hands and knees and reached to the back. The money was still there. She stuck the bag in her pocket and left the house, carrying the lamp.

She set the lamp on the porch, led the mare down to the barn, tied her up, and went into the barn. She added a little more feed for each animal, not knowing when they would be fed again. She checked the water buckets, knowing it would be too much for her, and decided it would have to be enough. She found a large can and filled it with kerosene. She carried the kerosene to the house and set it on the porch. She went into the house, picked up her father's field glasses from his desk, and slung them over her shoulder. She walked through the house one last time and noticed her mother's pearl comb. Her father had given it to her before Carly was born. She picked up the comb, put it in her pocket, took one last look around, and then went back outside. She thought about the short time her family had lived in the house. The small shack on the property was home until her father finished building this bigger, nice house. Her father was a carpenter in Ohio, so building the house was easy for him.

No reason to remember now. Everything she'd ever had, or ever known, was gone. She took the kerosene can, poured its contents on the porch and into the house, tossed the can inside, and picked up the lamp. She hesitated for a moment, and then pitched the lamp inside the house. The lamp broke and the kerosene ignited instantly. Flames grew higher and the walls of the building caught fire. When she knew the fire was hot enough, she turned and headed to the gray mare waiting at the barn. She stepped in the saddle and rode off, without looking back.

CHAPTER 4

Carly guided the mare onto the road and gave her free rein, knowing that she would stick to the road. It was dark when Carly finally reached the Circle J Ranch, and she only saw it because of the light from the house. Dogs were barking when she reined Brandy in at the ranch house. A middle-aged man came out of the door, hollered for the dogs to be quiet, walked to the edge of the porch, and peered into the darkness to see who was riding in.

"Mr. Johnson, this is Carly Barton. I need to talk to you."

"Oh, sure, Miss Barton. Climb down and come on in," he replied.

Carly dismounted, tied Brandy to the hitching rail and, with difficulty, she walked up the steps to the porch.

"Young lady, what are you doing out this time of night by yourself?" he asked with a scolding voice.

At the sound of her husband's voice, Alma Johnson came to the door. "Kendal Johnson, you stop hollering at that girl. Come on in, sweetheart, and tell us why you are here at this late hour."

Carly walked to the door and Mrs. Johnson put her arm around her shoulders as she led her inside the house. She looked at the girl. "Oh, my dear, what in the world happened to your face? Where's your clothes?" she asked.

"It's a long story, Mrs. Johnson, and I don't want to talk about it right now."

"All right, honey. Here, sit down and tell us how can we help you," the woman replied gently.

"I just want to find out if you can buy my land and my livestock," Carly replied, still standing.

"Your land? Where's your father? What happened?" asked Mr. Johnson.

"My parents are both dead. That's why I need to sell," she replied with tears streaming down her face.

Mrs. Johnson took her in her arms and held her for several minutes, then led her to the chair. "Oh, my dear, sit down, here's a hanky, and I'll get you some coffee, and something to eat. Kendal will take care of your horse. Won't you, dear?"

"I'll do it right now," replied the rancher. He hurried out of the room as if he was glad to get away.

"Mrs. Johnson, I'm in a hurry. I have to get to town and find a place to sleep," said Carly, agitated.

"Nonsense, young lady. You're going to sleep right here. You sit there until I can rustle up some food, and then you can tell us what happened to you and your parents," said Mrs. Johnson adamantly.

Carly sat in the chair and closed her eyes while Mrs. Johnson went to the kitchen to fix something for her to eat.

Several minutes later Mr. Johnson came in from stabling her horse. He looked over at the girl, went to the cupboard, and took out a bottle and two glasses. He poured two drinks, handed one to Carly, and sat down close to her. "Take a drink. It may help you."

"Mr. Johnson, I don't drink alcohol."

"Go on, drink. It will make you feel better."

She took a drink from the glass and choked on it. "I'm sorry."

"Don't apologize. It'll help calm your nerves. Now tell me why you want to sell your ranch," he said gently.

"I'm not going to live there anymore and your ranch is really close. I already burned the house, but the barn is solid, there are two horses, a cow, and some chickens. That must be worth something."

"Miss Barton, you have a nice piece of land and it is worth a lot more than I could afford to pay you. Besides, I'm getting old, and I don't want a large ranch."

He thought a moment, then asked, "Miss Barton, why did you burn the house? It was practically new."

She sipped the brandy again and it went down a little easier. She set the glass down on the table. "Mr. Johnson, please call me Carly."

"Okay, Carly, but this is also about money, and I don't have that much," he replied.

Mrs. Johnson came from the kitchen with a plate of food and a cup of hot coffee and handed it to Carly. She accepted the food and began to eat. Between mouthfuls she said, "I just want a few dollars and you can have everything."

"Carly, I can't take advantage of you and take your land for nothing," the rancher explained.

"Honey, why don't you just stay with us, and whenever you decide to go back, or sell the ranch, you'll have it," said Mrs. Johnson.

"I'm never going back to that ranch. I'm going after the three men who killed my parents, and I need money. I understand your situation. I'll get the money somewhere else," she said sternly.

"But honey, you're a woman, and a young one at that. You can't go after three killers by yourself," Mrs. Johnson said in a shocked voice.

"Mrs. Johnson, three men killed my parents, beat, and did awful things to me. It is my responsibility to hold them accountable. If you don't want to buy my ranch, I'll find someone else." She set her plate down and got out of the chair. "I'll be going now."

"Wait, Carly. Sit back down a minute. Look, I'll give you fifty dollars now, and you can stop at the Darby bank and get another hundred and fifty dollars. I'll take care of your ranch until you decide to come back. How would that be?" asked Mr. Johnson.

"That would be fine for me, but I won't be back," she answered.

"Things might look different down the road. You might change your mind," said the rancher.

"I don't think so —"

Mrs. Johnson interrupted, "Now, that's settled. Let me clean you up and you can stay in the spare room as long as you like."

"Thank you, but I had a bath before I left the ranch, and I'll be leaving early in the morning."

"Yes, you look reasonably clean, considering what you've been through, but a bath may help you sleep better. Come with me and we'll talk about your leaving in the morning," she suggested.

Mr. Johnson got fifty dollars from his desk and wrote a note to Edwin Olson at the Darby bank. He handed the money and the note to Carly before she disappeared into the bedroom. Mrs. Johnson brought a pan of warm water and a washcloth and asked her to take off her clothing. "Didn't you bring any dresses?"

"No, and I'm never going to wear a dress again," Carly replied angrily.

"Honey, you're a woman. You're supposed to wear dresses."

"I'm not a woman. That all disappeared when those three men showed up," she said bitterly.

Mrs. Johnson shook her head but did not reply. Instead, she examined Carly's injuries from head to toe, then washed her, and cleaned her wounds. Carly moaned a few times but mostly gritted her teeth as Mrs. Johnson rubbed salve on her cuts and bruises. Carly needed help to put on a nightshirt and was relieved to stretch out on the bed. Mrs. Johnson sat on the side of the bed and lightly rubbed the girl's head, neck, and shoulders, where there were no wounds. Carly moaned a bit as one tear slipped down her face. Mrs. Johnson said good night, and blew the light out on her way out of the door.

The woman's hands had been very soothing, and soon Carly fell asleep, but her sleep was disturbed. She did not know how long she had been asleep when she woke in a cold sweat, screaming. She rolled out of bed, curled up on the floor, and cried. Mrs. Johnson ran into the room carrying a lamp and knelt beside her.

The rancher's wife set the lamp down and put her arms around the frightened girl. "Everything is okay. You just had a bad dream," she said soothingly.

"They're attacking me!" sobbed Carly.

"You're all right now. Let's get you back in bed and I'll get you a glass of warm milk."

"No, please let me go into the kitchen with you."

"Everything okay in there?" asked Mr. Johnson from the hallway.

"Everything is all right, Kendal. Just go back to bed," replied Mrs. Johnson.

Mrs. Johnson got a robe for Carly and when she was covered, they went down the hall to the kitchen. By the time they reached the kitchen, Carly had calmed down considerably. Mrs. Johnson poured some milk in a pan and set in on the stove. A few minutes later, she poured two glasses of warm milk and jokingly said she should add some of her husband's brandy to it. That brought a smile to Carly's face, and the two women sat there chatting and drinking the milk.

Mrs. Johnson did most of the talking while Carly listened. About thirty minutes later they both went back to the bedroom. This time Mrs. Johnson left the lamp burning. Carly went back to bed and almost immediately fell asleep. She continued to have nightmares about the three men, especially the big man with the beard. She woke with a start when he put his hands around her neck. She sat up with a groan, but apparently, her tossing and turning did not wake the Johnsons this time.

CHAPTER 5

Carly woke several more times during the night, and finally, even though it was still early, she decided to get up. She dressed, although it was a painful process, and left the house. She appreciated the Johnsons' help, but she did not want to argue with them. She knew they would insist she stay with them, but she had a job to do.

She went to the barn, managed to saddle her horse, Brandy, mounted, and laid her father's rifle across her lap. Her destination was the town of Darby, Kansas, some five miles away. She had only been to town a couple of times, and she was not sure how to get there. She hoped that by heading south and staying on the main road, she would get close, or at least meet someone that could help her with directions.

What she did not realize was that there were not many people on this road this early, so she rode and rode, but saw no one.

She stopped at a creek and dismounted. She watered her horse and let her graze for a short while. She took a biscuit from her saddlebag, one that she had baked at the house, and ate it to hold off hunger pangs. Even though she had washed and bathed a couple of times, she still did not feel clean, and she hurt all over. She realized that her feelings and actions were controlled by her mind, but she could not stop thinking about the ordeal.

She stood her father's rifle against a sapling where she could easily reach it, then stripped naked. Now that the sun was up, she knew anyone riding by would see her, but at this point, she did not care. She got what she needed for a bath from her saddlebag and headed for the creek. The water was cold but she hardly noticed. She scrubbed, lathered, and scrubbed again, even though it was painful and sometimes blood stained the water. She still did not feel clean. Now she was sure she would never get rid of the scent of the outlaws or the feel of their hands on her. Even though she might not get rid of the men in her mind, she resolved to get revenge against them. She wanted to see them dead.

A few minutes later she walked out of the creek, allowed the sun to dry her, and she dressed. She picked up the rifle, mounted Brandy, and carrying the rifle across her lap, headed in the direction she believed would take her to Darby. She continued to ride having no idea how far she had traveled. Luck was with her and she finally reached town midmorning.

The biscuit was not enough to nourish her, and her body was demanding food. She had to buy some things, so lunch would have to wait until she found a store. As she rode down Darby's main street, she looked around town. She did not remember much about it from her earlier trips to town, but she did remember a general store. She should have no problem getting supplies that she needed there. When she found the store, she pulled her mare up in front, dismounted, tied her to the hitching rail in front of the store, and walked in.

Carly walked around, searching for supplies she needed, and when she noticed several women staring at her, she snapped, "What are you looking at?"

"Honey, young ladies should never wear men's clothing, and you need to put something on your face. Did you get kicked by a horse?" said one of the women.

Carly glared back at the woman. "Just mind your own business," she said angrily.

"Well, I never . . ." the woman stuttered. She turned and quickly left the store, followed by the others.

She forgot about the women and walked up to the counter.

"What can I do for you?" asked the man behind the counter, trying not to stare at her bruised face.

Carly handed the man a list of supplies. "I may need some other things. May I look around?"

The man examined the list. "You want a gun, holster, and cartridges?" he asked.

"Yes. That's what it says, doesn't it?"

"Yes, ma'am. I just meant . . ."

"I know what you mean. Can you fill the list or not?" Carly asked curtly.

The man stared at her, head to toe, "I can fill the order, if you have the money," he replied.

She pulled out the money Mr. Johnson had given her. "I've got money," she said. "I want everything sent over to the hotel as soon as possible."

"Yes, ma'am. Since you're a stranger here, you have to pay in advance, and I'll get it sent over to the hotel sometime this afternoon. Is that agreeable to you?"

"That'll be fine," she replied.

The man turned and busied himself filling

her order.

Carly walked over to the racks of clothing and began to look them over. After sifting through them for a while, she found a pair of men's pants and a shirt she thought would fit her and brought them to the counter.

"I want to take these with me now," she said.

The clerk came back to the counter and picked up the clothing. "Are these for you?" When she replied with an angry yes, he asked with surprise, "You know that these are men's clothing, don't you?"

"That's what I'm going to wear, and I don't give a damn who sees me wearing them."

"I'm sorry ma'am, I just meant —" He was no longer surprised, just unsure how to deal with this unusual and angry woman.

She interrupted him. "Just mind your own business," she replied curtly. She picked up the clothing and started for the door. She turned back to the man, "By the way, can you tell me where I can find someone who can teach me how to shoot?"

"What kind of shooting?" he asked, trying to understand.

Carly looked him in the eye. "I'm going to kill some men."

He stared at her for a moment. "You're serious."

"I'm dead serious."

"Who are you going to kill?"

"Killers. I've got money. I can pay, if that's a problem."

He hesitated, not sure, and then decided. "Clay Daggert is an old-time gunfighter. Well, actually, he's not that old. Anyhow, he always needs a little money. He might be able to help you."

"How do I find this Daggert person?"

"Well, he spends most of his time at the Red Rooster Saloon, drinking. It's not far from here, but they won't let you in."

"Thanks. I'll find it, and I'll worry about getting in later," she replied as she turned and left the store. She took her belongings from the mare and carried them into the nearby hotel.

When she walked in, she saw a young pimply man behind the counter. His face was so sharp it could split kindling. She decided that he must be about twenty or maybe a little older. She asked for a room.

"Are you alone?" he asked.

"That's none of your business, I just want a room. Do you have one or not?"

"I . . . didn't, I didn't mean to pry. We

always ask . . ." he stuttered. "Sure, we have rooms."

"All right, just give me the key and send some hot water up to the room so I can take a bath," she commanded him.

"Uh, ma'am, I have to collect payment up front, and you'll have to sign the register," he said nervously.

Carly put some coins on the counter and signed her name. "I'm going to be here for a week. Is that enough for the room and the bath?"

"Yes, ma'am. What you gave me will be fine," he replied with a weak smile.

"Is the dining room open?"

The young man read the name that she had written, "Yes ma'am, Miss Barton, just down the hall and through that door." He pointed.

"Thank you. Would you mind keeping some of my things here until I come back?"

"Yes, ma'am. I'd be glad to keep them behind the counter here. They'll be safe," he stuttered nervously.

She was not sure about him, but handed over her things, including her rifle, to the man and headed in the direction of the dining room. Even though she was hungry, she did not eat very much. Her mind was racing. She was not only in new surroundings, but everything was new or different from what she was used to, and she had a lot of planning to do. What she had to do was not going to be easy, but it was something she knew she must do. Finally, she left most of her food on her plate, paid at the counter, and left the dining room.

She stopped at the hotel desk, took her key, gathered her belongings, and carried them up the stairs to room four. She dropped the clothing and the rifle on the bed and lay down beside them. She had just dozed off when she heard a knock on the door. She went to the door and opened it. The young man from the desk was carrying a tin bathtub.

"Can I come in?" he asked.

She opened the door wider and let him in. He put the tub next to the bed. "I'll be back with the hot water," he said.

A few minutes later, he came back with two large buckets of hot water and proceeded to pour them in the tub. He smiled at Carly. "Enjoy your bath."

Carly did not respond and waited until he was gone. She removed her clothing and began to take her bath. She soaked for several minutes and then scrubbed her skin until it turned red. She stood, looked for the package from the general store, and realized it had not arrived. Taking a towel, she stepped out of the tub and dried herself off, then lay on the bed with just the towel covering her. Soon she was asleep. She dreamed that someone was knocking on the door and the big man with the beard was trying to choke her. She struggled to get away from him, and she woke up before he could kill her. She looked around the room and listened carefully, but there was no one around. She rolled over and, after some tossing and turning, she was able to go back to sleep. This time, there were no nightmares.

Carly did not wake up until late the next morning. She had not meant to sleep that long, but then remembered she did not have anything else to do until the bank opened. After washing up, she dressed in her new clothes and, as she was leaving, she noticed that the bathtub was gone. She had not locked her door. The noise that she heard during the night might have been someone picking up the tub. She shook her head, reminded herself to lock the door in the future, and then walked down the stairs.

The same young man stood behind the counter and smiled wickedly at her when she walked up. She had no doubt that the man was visualizing her naked, and was sure he had seen her on the bed last night. She decided she didn't give a damn but, her anger triggered, she vowed that no man was going to see her naked again.

"What can I do for you today, ma'am?"

"First of all, you can wipe that stupid grin off your face," she said.

"Yes, ma'am," he answered, quickly hiding his smile.

"Where can I find a man named Clay Daggert?" she asked.

"Daggert? What do you know about Clay Daggert?" His smile was replaced by surprise.

"I'm asking the questions, if you don't mind."

He looked at her for a moment. "I'm sorry, ma'am, but why in the world would you want to find Clay Daggert?" he asked incredulously.

"And just why shouldn't I find him?" she inquired mockingly.

"Ma'am, Daggert is a gunfighter, or at least he used to be. Now he's just a drunken bum."

"I don't care what he was, or is. I just want to talk to him."

The desk clerk shook his head and pointed to the right, "Well, if you really want to find him, he usually hangs out at the Red

Rooster Saloon, but it's early for him. He's probably sleeping off his drunk from last night. To get to the saloon, just go down to the corner, then turn right. It's in the middle of the block. You can't miss it."

"Thanks for your help," she replied. She handed him her key and went into the dining room. When she finished her breakfast, she left the hotel and found the bank. She gave the note from Mr. Johnson to Edwin Olson, the banker.

"Young lady, are you related to Mr. Johnson?" asked Olson.

"No, sir. I sold my ranch to him," she replied.

"And who would you be?"

"Carly Barton," she answered.

"Oh, yes. I remember your parents. I helped them buy their ranch." He smiled proudly.

"How are your parents?"

"They're both dead."

He looked at her strangely. "Both are dead?"

"Yes, and I don't want to talk about it."

"All right, but I'm sorry. I hope you got more for the ranch than this. I could have gotten you much more."

"It's not about the money. Besides, I had to sell it quickly."

"Well, if I can help you in any way, let me know. I'm sorry to hear about your parents." He gave her one hundred fifty dollars, and she left the bank. Her father had not liked the banker and, if he was sorry, it was probably because he lost another customer, she thought to herself.

She looked up and down the street and decided it was still too early to find Clay Daggert, so she went back to her hotel room.

A few hours later, Carly left the hotel, turned right, and followed the hotel clerk's directions until she found the saloon. Above the door was a large sign that read Red Rooster Saloon and above that was a painted picture of a red rooster. She looked around, did not see anyone, so walked up to the swinging doors and looked in. Four cowboys were playing cards at one table, but she did not see anyone that looked like a drunken bum. She stared at the bartender and waved her hand, trying to get his attention. When she was unable to, she pushed the doors open and walked in. Yes, her parents had warned her about saloons and gambling halls. Bad people hung around those places, but her parents were gone, killed by those same bad people that frequented those places. Besides, she did not want to wait around to find Clay Daggert.

The bartender stared at her as she walked up to the bar. "Ma'am, you shouldn't be in here." He spoke softly.

"That's what everyone tells me, but I need to find someone," she replied.

"You need to find someone from the saloon?"

"I was told that he spends most of his time in here. His name is Clay Daggert."

"Now, ma'am, why would you want to find Clay Daggert?" he asked curiously.

"Why does everyone ask me questions? If it's any of your business, I want to talk to him, and maybe have him do a job for me."

"Sorry, don't mean no harm, ma'am. I doubt he'd be interested in a job, but he's sitting at the table in the corner."

Carly looked but did not see him, until she realized the four cowboys were hiding a man behind them who was seated in a chair with his head on the table. All she could see was a head full of hair that was in desperate need of a haircut.

She pointed in the man's direction, and the bartender said, "Yep, that's him."

Carly started to walk toward the man but the bartender brought her up short saying, "Ma'am, you can't stay in here. Look, if you'll walk outside, I'll see if I can get him to come out and talk to you."

She hesitated for a moment, looking at the cowboys staring at her. She decided that his suggestion was a good one. The bartender came out from behind the bar and headed over to where the man was sitting. Carly turned and walked out of the saloon and waited on the porch. She waited, and waited, for what she thought was a long time, before the bartender finally came out.

"I'm sorry, ma'am, but he is barely awake, and he says he doesn't want to talk to anyone, especially a woman."

Carly thought about it for a moment. The man could probably use some money. She pulled ten dollars from her pocket. "Show him this, and see if he'll change his mind."

"Lady, I've got a saloon to run. I can't be running errands for you."

Carly looked at him. "Mr. Bartender, you have five men in your saloon and at least one doesn't give a damn if you're in there or not. I'm sure it won't overwhelm you to try one more time."

"All right, just this one time," he answered disgustedly. He took the money from her hand and headed back inside the saloon.

About five minutes later the bartender came out, holding Clay Daggert up to keep him from falling. Carly looked at the man close up. What she saw was not encouraging. His clothing was dirty and ragged. His hair was long and uncombed, and his face looked like he had not seen a razor in weeks or months. It was tough to figure his age in his condition. He might be about thirty-five or maybe some younger than that.

The bartender helped the man sit on a bench, and then handed the ten dollars back to Carly. "Lady, you're on your own. I have work to do," he said, and he went back inside the saloon.

She looked down at the man. "Are you the famous gunfighter?"

He glanced up at her through bloodshot eyes. "Don't know if I'm famous anymore. Who are you and what do you want?"

"I'm going to kill some men, and I need your help."

"Lady, it's going to cost you a lot more than ten dollars for me to kill someone."

"Mr. Daggert, I don't want *you* to kill anyone."

"Then why are you bothering me, if you don't want me to kill anyone?" he asked, putting his head in his hands.

"I just want you to teach me how to shoot." She handed him the ten dollars. "This is just the beginning, if you help me."

He took the money and put his head in

his hands again. "I need a drink."

"Mr. Daggert, it appears you've already had too many drinks. If I hire you, I need you sober."

"How'd you know if I'll work for a woman?"

"Mister, my money is as good as anyone's. Do you want the job or not?"

He looked up at her, ignoring her comment and her question. "You have a gun?"

"Yes, I have a rifle that I already know how to use. I also have a pistol. I want to learn how to shoot the pistol."

"You'd be better off shootin' someone with a rifle, if you really have to."

"What do you mean?" she asked.

"Use a rifle, and they'd be much farther away, an' you'd be safer."

"I don't want to be safer," she stated.

"Now I don't understand, an' my head is killin' me."

"I can't help your headache, but I'll explain my problem. I need help learning to shoot a pistol so I can look in their eyes when I shoot them." Carly began to feel frustrated.

"I can't help you. I have no interest in helpin' you get killed; besides I need a drink."

"Keep the ten, and I've got forty more

dollars. If you sober up, and remember me, come to the hotel, and the clerk will call me. If I don't hear from you in a couple of days, I'll find someone else." She turned and headed back to the hotel.

Daggert stared at her until she turned the corner, then he went back into the saloon.

Carly rounded the corner and ran into a man.

"Sorry, ma'am, I guess I turned the corner too quick."

She stepped back and looked at him. He was a big man, close to fifty, with a paunch, and he was wearing a badge on his chest. "That's okay," she said and attempted to walk past him.

"Sorry, ma'am. I'm Marshal Sam Warlock, and I need a word with you."

"What do you need to talk to me about?"

"Mr. Gordon at the general store said that you're trying to hire a gunfighter."

"I am, but I don't see how that's any of your business."

"Look, young lady, I'm the marshal here. So any mention of gunfighters is my business. Now, tell me why you're trying to hire a gunfighter. Say, aren't you the Barton girl?"

"Yes, I'm Carly Barton."

"Where are your parents?"

"They're dead."

"Dead? What happened to them?"

"They were killed, in our house, by three escaped convicts from Kansas State Prison that you and the prison guards should've caught before they killed my parents."

"How'd you know they were convicts?" he asked.

"They told me. They weren't trying to hide it."

"I'll ride out to your ranch and investigate. I'd appreciate it if you'd come by later and help me finish up the paperwork."

"What good would that do for my parents, if you go out and investigate?" she answered angrily.

"Ma'am, the law can't be everywhere. Yes, I received a telegram that four men attempted an escape from prison. The authorities wounded and captured one escapee only a few miles from the prison. Prison officials thought the other three were heading in a different direction than here. When did it happen?"

"Look, Marshal, I understand that you're trying to help, but I don't want or need your help," she replied.

"Young lady, murder and gunfighters are my job. Now you're trying to hire a gunfighter to do my job," he answered, his voice rising.

"Marshal, you can do what you want to with the convicts, if you can find them. But if I find them first, they will be dead. Anyhow, I'm *not* trying to hire anyone to do my killings."

"So please tell me, if you're not looking to hire a gunman, why're you asking about Clay Daggert?"

"That's my business, but I'll tell you anyway. I'm looking for someone to teach me how to handle a gun. After that, I plan to track down the men who raped me and killed my parents."

"You know, revenge can get you in a lot of trouble. You can get yourself killed, or be arrested, whether you hire someone or you do it yourself. Besides, what makes you think that someone like Clay Daggert can teach you how to use a gun? Even if he can, he could get in trouble for aiding and abetting a murder," the marshal said sternly.

"Marshal, I have nothing else to say to you. If you want to arrest me, you are free to do so. If not, stay out of my business." She quickly moved past him and headed for the hotel.

Marshal Warlock watched her walk down the sidewalk. Yes, he probably could have taken her in and tried to persuade her to allow the law to deal with the convicts, but this was one angry and determined woman. Maybe later she would come to her senses. He shook his head and walked on down the street to his office.

Sometime later, Clay Daggert staggered into Woodley's Boarding House. Mrs. Woodley was waiting for him when he came through the door.

"H-he-hello, Mrs. Woodley," he stuttered.

"Don't hello me, Mr. Daggert. You have been promising to pay your bill for several days."

He took two steps forward, almost falling. "My word is good. I'm gonna pay soon."

"Not soon, now. You've been sleeping and eating here for two months and you've only paid me five dollars. I can't afford to keep anyone that doesn't pay their bills, especially someone that drinks and gambles up all of his money."

He pulled out some bills from his pants pocket and handed them to her.

"Three dollars, that's not nearly enough," she replied.

"I've only got a couple more dollars and I need it for . . . for . . ."

She interrupted, "You mean for liquor?"

"Now Mrs. Woodley, I've . . ."

"Forget it. You haven't spent any money on anything other than whiskey for days, or maybe even weeks. You haven't shaved in days, even though I gave you one of my late husband's razors, and I have no idea when you last had a haircut."

"But Mrs. Woodley —"

"I haven't finished yet," she interrupted. "When was the last time you bought any decent clothing?"

"Can't, if you don't have a job or money."

"You are hopeless. I don't know why I even put up with you."

He pulled out another dollar and handed it to her.

"Did you finally get a job, or did you steal this money?" she asked, putting the four dollars in her apron pocket.

"Well, sorta."

"Gambling money or a job, either way, does it mean you can pay your bills from now on?"

"I'm goin' to try."

"Aw shucks, just go to bed, and when I see you for breakfast in the morning, I expect you to at least be clean-shaven." She turned on her heel and walked away.

"Yes ma'am, I'll do it," he answered as he staggered up the stairs to his room.

CHAPTER 6

As Carly walked toward the hotel, she was boiling mad. The marshal had no right to lecture her. Her plans, and whom she talked to, were her own business. She was going to get revenge on the three men who killed her parents and raped her, if it was the last thing that she ever did. No one, not even the marshal, was going to stop her.

She was still seething when she reached the counter at the hotel. "Hello, Miss Barton," said the smiling young man, behind the counter.

Carly cut him short. "My key, please."

"Yes, ma'am, right away," he replied as the smile on his face disappeared.

He turned, took the key from the box, and handed it to her. "Anything else I can get you?"

"When does the dining room open?"

"About a half an hour from now," he said, a small smile returning.

"Thanks," she said and headed toward the stairs.

"Oh, I delivered a package to your room from the general store. I hope you don't mind," the young man added.

She stopped at the bottom of the stairs, turned toward him, nodded, and as she turned back to go upstairs, noticed an elderly couple sitting in the lobby. They were staring at her, and her hand automatically lifted to the bruises on her face. She hurried on up the stairs to her room. Those old folks were probably looking at her face, or maybe the way she was dressed, but either way, she did not care. Everyone would just have to get used to the way she looked and the way she dressed.

Carly reached her room and opened the door. On the bed in front of her was the package from the store the clerk was supposed to have delivered yesterday. She immediately tore open the package and checked the contents to see if she received everything she ordered. After she was satisfied, she picked up the gun and holster and wrapped the belt around her waist. The belt was much too long for her. She had noticed a gun shop when she rode into town. She was sure the gun-shop man could shorten the belt and punch some new holes in it for her.

She heard a knock on her door. "Who is it?" she asked loudly.

"The desk clerk. I brought you some fresh water and some towels."

"Come in. The door's not locked," she said as she remembered that locking her door would be a good idea from now on.

The man came in carrying a pail of water and two towels. "Sorry to disturb you. I know we have not met, but my name is Hugh Duffy. I thought you might want some fresh water to wash up with . . . you have a gun," he stammered.

"What's the matter, Hugh Duffy? You've never seen a gun before?" Her voice dripped sarcasm.

"Well no. I mean yes. I mean not a big gun," he stuttered.

"What you mean is, you have never seen a woman carrying a gun like this."

He shook his head. "I'll just put the water on the washstand."

"That will be fine. Thank you."

Hugh looked at the gun belt and the gun again, hurried out of the room, and quickly closed the door. Carly locked the door, dropped the gun belt on the bed, and held the gun in her right hand. It was heavier than she thought it would be. She had never handled a pistol. Her father had owned a shotgun at one time, but he sold it for the trip west. He owned a rifle, the one she had now. She remembered shooting the shotgun once when she was about fifteen, and it almost knocked her on her butt. From that time on, she only fired the rifle, and she was good with it.

She laid the gun on the bed, picked up the pail of water, and poured water into the washbowl. She washed her hands and face, and then dried off. She forgot about the dining room, lay across the bed, and soon fell asleep. Some hours later, noises in the street woke her and she got up to look out the window. It was dark, and she could only see a handful of people. No supper for her, she decided, and went back to bed.

In the morning, Carly walked into the dining room for breakfast and the first person she saw was Clay Daggert. She was surprised that he was up, considering the state he was in yesterday. He was sitting at a table by himself, his face washed, his hair somewhat combed, and his face shaved. Other than that, he looked the same as he did yesterday in front of the saloon. She headed directly to his table and stopped in front of him.

"May I sit down?" she asked politely.

Clay Daggert looked up at her with blood-shot, unrecognizing eyes. "Suit yourself. It's not my table."

"You're an arrogant bastard."

He was taken aback. No one talked to him like that, much less a woman. "Lady, what do you want from me?"

"First of all, I want to sit down, with your permission," she replied.

He looked her up and down and then muttered, "So go ahead and sit down. I don't care."

Carly pulled out the chair, sat, and waited for someone to take her order. When that was over, she asked, "Mr. Daggert, have you considered my offer?"

"What offer?" he asked gruffly, surprised again by this woman.

"You don't even remember talking to me yesterday, in front of the saloon, do you?"

"Lady, I don't even know you, much less remember a conversation yesterday."

"Well, I must say you look some better now than you did yesterday. Was that my money you used to clean yourself up?"

"I don't know about your money, but I do sober up a little this time of day so that I can get drunk again tonight." He smirked. "As for your question, I seem to remember

81

a woman yesterday. Don't remember no offer."

A man brought her coffee and Carly continued. "My offer was for me to pay you to teach me how to shoot a pistol." Her voice was curt, businesslike, confident, and determined.

He looked at her incredulously. "Lady, you got to be kidding. Why would I want to do that anyway?"

Carly was deadly earnest when she looked him in the eye without flinching and said, "No Mr. Daggert, I'm not kidding, and you didn't think so either when you took my ten dollars. I hear that you are, or were, an expert with a pistol, and I want you to teach me how to be the same."

Daggert stared across at her for a moment. "What makes you think that I'm an expert with a gun? I don't remember taking your ten dollars."

"I've spoken to a couple of people in town and they tell me you are, or were, the best around. And yes, you did take my money, and I can prove it if necessary."

He lifted his right hand, ran it through his bushy hair, and then pointed his finger at her. "See my hand shake? You think I can shoot with that?"

"I'm sure you could, if you lay off the

whiskey for a while, and you might even remember what is going on in your life. Besides, I don't plan for you to shoot anyone. I'm going to do the shooting."

He rubbed his face and looked at her. "I'm pretty busy these days."

"You spend your days and nights in a saloon. You've got all the time in the world."

He forced a smile. "You're a snoop. Is that what you do for a living? You are wrong about one thing. I spend most of my days sleeping over at Mrs. Woodley's boarding house."

She looked at him and decided he had a nice smile, but she said, "Sleeping off your drunken spells. Anyway, as I said, I talked to a couple of people about you, and they say you are the best. I want the best, and I'm willing to pay good money."

Daggert raised his arm to get the attention of the waiter. The man walked over, refilled their coffee cups, and said, "Miss, your breakfast will be out in a moment."

She nodded, and then turned to Daggert as she sipped her hot coffee. "If you're living in a boarding house, why aren't you eating there?"

"I get tired of eating there. Sometimes I want a change."

"You mean when you get extra money?"

She watched him and waited for him to respond.

He ignored her last question as he sipped his coffee. "Who are you going to shoot?"

"That's my business, not yours," she answered curtly.

He leaned closer, and Carly could smell alcohol on his breath. "Lady, who do I have the pleasure of —"

"My name's Carly Barton. I introduced myself to you yesterday."

"I don't remember, but Mrs. or Miss Barton, I live by a strict code. I can't help you unless you tell me who you're planning to shoot."

She shook her head, "It's Miss, and just what strict code is that?" she asked.

"I always know who, and why, I kill a man."

"If you don't have to shoot anyone, and I tell you who I plan to shoot, then you will help me?"

"I don't know that for sure, but I do know that I will not help you, if you don't tell me."

She considered it for a moment, "Okay, I'll tell you." She began the story, stopped for a few minutes to eat, and then started again.

When she finished, Clay Daggert looked

at her. "I'm sorry you had to go through that, but why not speak to the marshal? He's a good man."

"Mr. Daggert, let me ask you a question."

"Shoot," he replied, then grinned over his response.

"Yes, shoot is right. Would you tell the marshal if something like this happened to you or someone you know?" she asked, looking directly into his eyes.

"But lady, this is different, I'm a —"

"Mr. Daggert," she interrupted, "If you're going to tell me that you are a man and I'm a woman, don't, because I don't give a damn. I'm going to take care of my own problems, and if you don't want to help me, I'll find someone who will." She scooted her chair back and stood up. As she started to walk away, Daggert put his hand on her arm.

"Sit back down, Miss Barton. I didn't say I wouldn't help you."

Reluctantly she sat back down.

"Now, you don't want to hire a gunman, is that right?" he asked.

"Mr. Daggert, I've tried to explain this before. No. I'm not interested in hiring a gunfighter. I just want to find someone to teach me how to shoot straight and fast," she replied, shaking her head.

"You're going to be a gunman?" he asked incredulously.

"A gunwoman, and just why would that surprise you?"

"Well, you must admit it's a most unusual occupation for a wom . . . uh, a young lady."

"So is being a prizefighter, or whatever they're called!" Carly said, thoroughly annoyed. "But I hear there are several women who have taken up that unsavory occupation and many men have flocked to the ring to see them take a beating. I doubt whether any of those men would say that it's an unusual occupation."

Daggert sat with his mouth open, listening to the woman justify the occupation she wanted to get into. "So, do you know any of those 'prizefighters'?"

"I know of several, including Elizabeth Stokes and Bruising Peg. They fought early in the 1700s. Of course, there was the fight between Mary Ann Fielding and the Jewess. That match went over eighty minutes and there were seventy knockdowns. Then there was The Boxing Baroness, Lady Barrymore."

Daggert smiled. "Yes, and I understand they boxed bare-breasted."

"Why not? Men do," she snapped back.

His smile disappeared and he decided to

drop the subject and explore another avenue. "Let me see your hands."

"What?" she asked, still annoyed.

"Just show me your hands."

She glared at him for a moment, then slowly lifted her hands, and he took hold of them.

"Right- or left-handed?"

"What does that matter?"

"It matters about as much as your diatribe on women prizefighters. Just answer the question."

Her face flushed and she started to yell at him but her need for his help won out. "I'm right-handed," she replied.

Daggert dropped her left hand and examined her right. "Your hand is rather small," he observed.

"And what does that mean?"

"That means your hand has to be big enough to hold a gun, and fire it, with one hand, if you want to be a gunman. Do you have a gun?"

"Yes, I have a gun. I have a rifle that belonged to my father, and I have a pistol that I bought here in town."

"Can you use the rifle?"

"Yes, I'm a good shot with the rifle."

"Then why don't you use the rifle to kill those men?"

"You may not understand this, but I need to kill them up close. I want to see them die, rather than ambush them from a distance."

"What difference will it make? If you get a chance to shoot them, they'll still be dead."

"What they did to me and my parents, they did close up, and I'm going to do the same thing. I want to see it in their eyes when they die," she said.

"Okay, what kind of gun did you buy?"

"It's a pistol."

"Lady, there's lots of pistols, all different. Can you tell me the make or model?" he asked her.

"No. It's just a handgun," she said, embarrassed by her lack of knowledge.

"I'll tell you what I'll do. Tomorrow afternoon I'll meet you at the flats, and we can see if you can shoot the gun."

"Where are the flats?" she asked.

"Oh, you're not from around here. The flats are a mile or so west of here. Take the main road out of town until you reach a small creek, then turn north. It'll be only a few hundred yards and you'll find some boulders and a grove of cottonwoods."

"What time?"

"How about one o'clock? By the way, you have a horse?"

"Yes, I have a horse and I'll meet you there. Are you going to be sober then?" she asked.

"I can't promise that, but I can tell you that I'm heading to the saloon now. I really need a drink. How about an advance?"

"You didn't say you would take the job. I gave you ten dollars, and you already forgot that. Tell me why I should give you another advance," she demanded with a frown.

"I'm meeting you tomorrow, which should be worth something," he replied with a hint of a smile on his face.

"All right, but you better show up, and you had better be sober," she said skeptically. She pulled out some coins and handed them to him.

"Much obliged ma'am. I'll see you tomorrow. Bring ammunition, and you had better have some money, because it'll cost you a lot."

"I'll buy the ammunition, and I've got the money. Don't you worry about that."

He nodded and headed for the door. Carly watched him walk out, unsteady on his feet, but steadier than yesterday, and she shook her head. She sure hoped she was not making a big mistake, hiring a drunk.

She finished her food quickly, left the dining room, and went to her room. She picked up the gun belt and visited the gun shop. The man adjusted the belt to fit her narrow hips. She paid him and left the shop. He had asked no questions and didn't seem to think it strange that he should be asked to fit a woman. She returned the gun belt to her room, and then spent the next couple of hours walking around town. She looked at people, especially men, trying to learn facial details. She got many stares, some inquisitive and others downright ugly, but she did not care — she had a job to do and it did not matter whether she was liked or not.

CHAPTER 7

The next afternoon Carly buckled on her gun belt, and following Daggert's directions, rode to the flats where she was to meet him. She dismounted, watered her mare, Brandy, in the nearby creek, and waited impatiently for the gunman to appear. It seemed like a long time, and she was beginning to think he was not going to come, when she heard a horse. She watched Daggert until he reined in.

"Howdy, Miss Barton," he greeted her cheerfully.

She stared at him without acknowledging his greeting.

He decided that she was a woman on a mission. He could not read her thoughts, so he decided to do what he always did when he was not sure of a situation. He kept his mouth shut.

"Mr. Daggert, I'm paying for your services. I expect you to do what I want, and when I want. If you can't do that, just tell me and I'll find someone else."

People did not talk to him like that. Daggert was taken aback by her harshness, and didn't have an idea how to take her.

"Ma'am, I'm only a few minutes late. I —"

Carly interrupted him. "Let's just get started. We've wasted enough time already." She turned and walked over to a large rock. She took off her hat, laid it on the rock, and faced him.

"What do I do first?" she asked.

"Is that gun you're carrying loaded?" he asked.

"Yes."

"Unload it."

She looked bewildered, "Why?"

"So you won't shoot yourself, or me."

She reluctantly unloaded the gun, holstered it, put the bullets in her pocket, and looked expectantly at him.

"All right, pull the gun and point it at that small bush to your right."

She did what he commanded, and when the gun cleared the holster, it dropped to the ground. She cursed under her breath.

"That's okay. Try it again. It'll take you awhile. Take it slow until you get used to it," Daggert encouraged her.

For the next hour, Carly pulled the gun from its holster, pointed it, and then let it slip back into her holster.

"When do I get to shoot the gun?"

"Be patient. I know you're tired. Let's stop for now. We can continue tomorrow."

"There's no time to waste. I want you to teach me all the skills that made you successful."

"Look, lady, women aren't born to be gunslingers."

If looks could kill, he would have been gutted and would have bled out, and he knew it. He waited patiently and curiously to hear her response.

"Mr. Daggert, nobody is born to be a gunslinger. Nobody is supposed to kill, and nobody is supposed to die at the hands of another man."

"I suppose you're right —"

She interrupted him. "But some do . . . kill and die."

Daggert started to speak, but realized she was not finished, so he waited.

Carly looked directly at him. "Don't ever say to me that women are not supposed to do anything. Women are born to live and have dreams just like men. They're no different."

Daggert shifted from one foot to another

nervously. He had faced many men, and killed his share, but facing this woman was somehow different. He just waited for her to continue.

"Do you understand that?"

"I'm afraid I can't argue with you on that."

"All right, then let's get back to practicing. I don't have much time."

Daggert had thought that after Carly spent some time practicing with the six-gun, she would change her mind, but that was not happening. She was forging ahead with even more determination.

"Appears you have your mind made up," he said.

"Glad you finally see it my way. I'm going to practice some more."

"I'll bet you would be a hell of a poker player," he said with a grin.

"You know anything about gambling?" she asked curiously.

"I've played a lot of games of chance," he replied.

"Are you any good? Could you teach me how?"

"I certainly can teach you the basics, but why would you want to gamble?"

"It could help me make money, and it might help me find the killers. I'm sure they'll frequent saloons where there's gambling."

"Miss Barton, not many people win a lot of money while gambling, unless they are a professional gambler, and sometimes even they lose."

"We'll talk about gambling later, but now let's get back to the gun."

"Yes, ma'am."

She continued to practice until her hand got so sore she could not pull the gun from the holster. She thought she had made some progress, but Daggert told her she was far from being good enough to face anyone with a gun.

"Before we go any farther, you need to be able to clean the gun. Failure to do so could cause a misfire. The other thing you need to learn is how to load and reload quickly. You never know when you may need another set of rounds."

"Anything else?" she asked.

"Yes, forget about this fool notion and get on with your life."

She glared at him until he looked away.

"I was told the only smart gunfighter is a dead one," he said.

"Dead? What do you mean? The only smart gunfighter is the dead one?"

"Well, when a man, or a woman," he hastily added, "accepts he's already dead, he's got nothing to lose. That makes him free. He's not afraid of dying, so he can do anything he wants."

"That fits me. I might as well be dead," she answered.

"Well, in that case, I'd suggest you talk to Ed Wirthing at the gun shop. He may be able to fix the gun to fit your smaller hand."

"What's wrong with my small hands?"

"Nothing, but it just might be easier for you to draw and shoot if the grips were a little smaller, so the gun fits your hand better," he explained.

"Anything else I need to know?"

"There're plenty more, but for the time being, keep plenty of bullets in your belt, and shadow practice when you can."

"What does that mean?"

"Unload the gun and practice drawing in front of a mirror."

"Okay, I'll practice when I get back to the hotel. We'll meet the same time tomorrow," she said sternly.

To Daggert it was a demand, and he normally did not react positively to demands, but Miss Barton was not the usual woman. "Yes, ma'am. The same time tomorrow, and the same place."

"Mr. Daggert, since we are going to be

working together for a while, you may call me Carly."

"Yes, ma'am, I mean, Carly."

Without any further conversation, she turned, walked to Brandy, and mounted. "And make sure you're sober when we meet."

"I'll try. You know, I may need some extra money for expenses," he hollered.

"Our deal is for fifty dollars and not a cent more."

Clay Daggert turned his head away and mumbled to himself, "Why the hell am I putting up with such a difficult woman?"

"Did you say something?" she asked.

"No, ma'am, no. I didn't say anything," he lied.

She stared at him for a moment, then turned Brandy and headed back to town.

CHAPTER 8

Kirby Wilson could not wait to rid himself of the other two convicts. It had been several days since the three men broke out of prison, and he had been their slave the entire time. Sure, he was younger than the other two, but he helped plan the prison break, helped steal the horses, and then helped them find the farmhouse. He thought they would ask for food and water and then move on, but they wanted everything. He was only twenty-four, and he had killed his share of men, but he did not hold to killing women and old men. He was sure they could have gotten what they wanted without killing those two farmers. And then raping that young woman. He had a feeling they had not seen the last of her. As feisty as she was, she just might try to make good on her promise to get even.

All his killings had been face to face, with the other man having a gun, and able to shoot back. Unfortunately, his last killing was a bank guard. He and two other men tried to rob a bank in Caldwell, Kansas, and the episode ended badly. When they turned to leave the bank, the guard shot one of his companions in the back. Kirby had to kill the guard in self-defense. His other partner escaped, but he did not. He was shot out of the saddle trying to help his wounded partner. He had thought about that several times over the last four years while he was lying on a cot in prison. He cursed himself for being so stupid. He would never put himself in that position again. He could have gotten away, except he was too loyal for his own good.

He met Wes Stone and Rod Ulrich in state prison a couple of days after arriving on the prison wagon. He found Stone to be mean, devious, and a dangerous bully, and Rod Ulrich his crony. Ulrich produced very few original thoughts, so he took his cues from Stone.

Kirby mostly kept his distance from the two men during his prison time, until his cellmate encouraged him to come in with them and plan an escape. Unfortunately, his cellmate took a bullet and died during the escape. Kirby was sure it was Stone's fault because he wasted valuable time trying to get even with one of the guards.

His thoughts were interrupted when Stone hollered, "Kirby!" He reined in and looked at the big man. "What've you been thinkin' 'bout?" asked Stone.

"Nothin' important," replied Kirby.

"All right. I said we're going to set up camp over near the creek bed," said the big man.

"Okay with me." Kirby did not really care where they camped, because where they were did not appear to have any nearby towns.

They rode another couple hundred yards, reined in, and dismounted. Stone stretched, trying to get the kinks out of his body. "Kirby, gather some wood and build a fire. Rod, take care of the horses and make sure they don't get too much water too soon."

Rod immediately took the reins of the horses and headed for the creek. Kirby stared at the big man for a moment, decided now was not the time to challenge him, and then headed out to find some wood. None of the men cooked very well, but Kirby was the youngest, so that job became his too. He gathered enough firewood, built a fire, and began to cook. He did the best he could with the beans and bacon and then made coffee. He dished out his own food, walked a few feet away, and sat down on the creek bank to eat.

"Kirby, how're we supposed to eat this slop?" asked Stone.

The young man turned and stared at the man a few moments. "If you don't like my cooking, do it yourself."

"And the coffee tastes like it was made of sawdust," added Rod.

"Shut up, Ulrich. This is the last cooking I'll do for you, so you can cook yourself, or starve. You choose," snapped Kirby as he threw down his plate and tin cup and stood.

Kirby could hear Stone yelling at him, but he ignored him, and walked until he was in the trees and out of sight of the camp. He sat on the ground, rolled a cigarette, and stared up at the darkening sky. After an hour or so, he stood and walked over to where the horses were. He made sure they were securely tied before walking back to the camp. The other two men were already asleep, so he pulled off his boots, unbuckled his gun belt, and slid under his blanket. He kept the gun close to his right hand. He was not comfortable sleeping close to the other convicts.

Just before light, Kirby woke in a cold sweat. He was hearing a woman's screams, and he saw the vague figure of his father carrying a long black whip. Even though he had left home many years ago, he could not shake this recurring nightmare. This time he could not decide if the screams were coming from his mother or the women at the farmhouse.

During his boyhood, Kirby's father used a whip on him many times before he decided to run away. His mother would try to save him from the whippings, but usually she got beat up by his father's fist. She died when he was twelve, and a year later he ran away.

He slipped from under the blanket, pulled on his boots, and picked up his gun belt. He put on the gun belt as he walked to the horses. He leaned against a tree, and his mind wandered back to the day he left home. His father came home drunk from town and hit him. This time it was because he was not finished with his chores. It did not matter though, because his father never needed a reason to beat him. That was the last time, because at the age of thirteen, he simply walked away and never went back.

"Kirby, where are you?"

His thoughts interrupted, he silently cursed Stone as he walked back to camp.

"Boy, get some breakfast fixed so we can get riding," said Stone.

"Stone, I told you last night, I'm not cooking for you. Let your errand boy do it."

"Hey, kid, who you calling an errand boy?" asked Rod.

Stone glared at Kirby for a few moments. "Never mind, Kirby. Rod, see if you can rustle up some grub so we can get on the road."

Kirby walked away in search of firewood. He could not wait to reach Rock Springs and rid himself of these two men.

CHAPTER 9

Carly rode back to town from the flats, dropped off her mare at the livery stable, and stopped at the gun shop. The owner, working on a rifle, looked up when she walked inside. "Howdy, ma'am. Need some more adjustment on that belt, or might I help you with something else?" he asked.

"Yes, my name is Carly Barton. Clay Daggert said you might be able to help me."

"I'm Ed Wirthing, but everyone just calls me Ed. What kind of help do you need today?"

"Well Ed, Daggert thought you might be able to fix this gun so it will fit my hand better."

"You a friend of Clay's?" he asked.

"No, just a business acquaintance."

The man looked at her and smiled. "Well, ma'am, I know Clay Daggert, and he doesn't do much for free, even for friends. Anyway, let me see the gun."

Carly handed him the gun and let him examine it before she spoke. "Can you fix it for me?"

"Well, I could, but it would take some time and maybe cost more than it's worth." He thought a moment. "I have a gun I can trade you, and I think it will fit you much better than this one."

"I want a good, reliable gun, not just something you have stored in the back room," she said firmly.

"Oh, no, ma'am. This is a fine gun." He stood, walked to the wall, and took a gun from the shelf. "Now this gun was custom-made for a smaller grip. It has a shaved barrel and raised hammers. The grips were custom-fit for a smaller than average hand."

He spun the cylinder and smiled. "It ticks as quietly and easily as a Swiss clock." He handed the gun to Carly.

She took it, inspected it carefully, slid it in her holster, and then pulled it out. The gun did fit her hand better, and it came out easier than her gun. "It feels really good. You have ammunition for this one?"

"Sure," he replied as he pulled out a box from the counter. "Now I need to warn you, this gun has a hairpin trigger, so be very careful how you handle it, and who you point it at."

"Oh, I'll be very careful about who I point it at. Better make that two boxes. Even swap?" she asked.

"Even swap, and I'll even throw in the shells."

"Both boxes?" she asked.

"Yes, both boxes. By the way, I have a very nice derringer. You can hide it under your clothing, just in case."

"Just in case what?"

"If your pistol isn't close by, or you just need a second gun." He pulled out the small gun and handed it to her. She was not thrilled about using a hidden gun. When she killed her attackers, she wanted them to know who she was and why she was killing them. However, what Mr. Wirthing said made sense. This one could always be in her pocket, if she ran into trouble.

"Okay, I'll take it." Without haggling over the price, she took the derringer and the shells for it, and paid for them. "Thanks for your help."

"Good luck, Miss Barton, and listen to Daggert. He's one smart *hombre* when it comes to guns, or people."

She started to say, "He's also a drunk," but kept her silence. She slipped the derringer and the ammunition in her pocket. "That's still to be seen."

Wirthing frowned as he watched her head for the door, but he did not say anything. She was an odd and very determined young woman.

After leaving the gun shop, Carly went to her hotel room. She took a nap, then freshened up. Before she headed downstairs to the dining room, she pulled out the derringer and made sure it was loaded. She dropped it into her pocket and left the box of ammunition in the room.

She walked into the dining room and immediately became aware of the eyes of all present staring at her. She knew a woman by herself, with a black and blue face, and wearing men's clothing, was an unusual sight. Everyone would talk about her. For a moment, she thought about asking the kitchen to send her food to her room, but then her temper flared. To hell with these people. *They do not know me, I do not know them, and I do not want to know them.* She stared straight ahead as she walked to an empty table and sat down.

The waiter came to her table, took her order, and brought Carly some coffee. She had just taken a couple of sips when she saw the marshal come through the dining room door. He saw her and walked to her table.

"Miss Barton, may I join you?"

"Suit yourself. It's your town," she replied without looking at him.

He sat down and hesitated for a moment before speaking. "Miss Barton, I didn't mean to rile you. I know how difficult this situation must be for you."

"Marshal, I don't think you have any idea about what I'm going through. If you did, and if you were truly a real man, then you'd do the same thing I'm doing."

"I guess you're right. I certainly cannot relate to what happened to you." He hesitated and then continued. "I understand you're doing some shootin' practice."

"Is there a law against shooting practice?" she asked.

"No law against shootin' practice. Ma'am, I'm not trying to cause you trouble. I'm tryin' to keep you out of it."

She looked at the marshal. "I can take care of myself, if you don't mind."

"Look, Miss Barton, the escaped prisoners, as you already know, are killers. You were lucky they didn't kill you."

"So now you're telling me I'm a lucky woman, and I should just forget it?"

"I'm just saying —"

She interrupted him. "I am not lucky. They did kill the real me, and their mistake was not finishing me off, because now I intend to track them down and kill them, all three of them."

"Ma'am, if you don't mind my saying so, you have as much a chance of finding those men as you have of snaring a wisp of smoke on a windy day."

"Then if you are so sure I can't find them, why are you worrying about me?"

"My concern is that they'll find you, if you go on asking too many questions. They won't hesitate to shoot someone from an alley. They're all back-shooters. All I want is for you to let the law deal with them."

"The law had them and let them go. That's why my parents are dead. I won't let them get away when I find them."

"Do you know where they went when they left your house?" he asked.

"I already told you. I don't know where they were going, but I'm going to find out."

"I'm sorry I'm making you angry, but I'm not sure you told me the whole truth. You're going out to look for them, so you must have some direction in mind."

"Sorry I can't help you, Marshal," she replied as her food came. "Now, if you will excuse me, I'm going to eat my dinner."

The marshal stood, turned to leave, and then turned back to Carly. "It's my job to warn you that you're getting yourself into a lot of trouble," he said gruffly.

"Thanks for the warning," she answered with more than a hint of sarcasm in her voice.

Marshal Sam Warlock shook his head and left the dining room. Their conversation had attracted attention, and Carly angrily stared down several of the other customers before she turned back to her food. When she was finished eating, she went back to her room. For the next hour, she practiced in front of the mirror drawing her new pistol from her holster.

CHAPTER 10

The next day, a few minutes before one o'clock, Carly reached the flats and was surprised to find Clay Daggert already waiting there. "Afternoon, ma'am," he said as she dismounted.

"Good afternoon, Mr. Daggert," she replied.

"You ready to do some real shootin'?" he asked.

"With real bullets I hope," she answered.

"Yes, real bullets today."

Carly stared at him. He was clean-shaven and his hair was trimmed. He was wearing the same trousers as before, but he had on a new shirt. Her first observation from the other day was correct. Clay Daggert was a handsome man.

"Something wrong?" he asked quizzically.

She blushed in spite of herself. "No, nothing is wrong," she replied as she walked over to the spot where she had practiced yesterday.

"Looks like you got a new gun. Is it loaded?" Daggert asked.

"No, I have not loaded it yet." She handed the gun to Daggert, and he examined it carefully. "Custom-made. Should fit your hand much better. Hairpin trigger. You'll have to be very careful."

"It does feel better. I traded my old one, even up, for this one." She thought about telling him about the derringer but decided not to. Mr. Wirthing would probably tell him anyway.

"I'd say you made a very good trade. You have bullets?"

"In my saddlebag. I'll go get them."

"Never mind. I'll get them. You go ahead and start practicing your quick draw," he said as he handed back the gun.

"Quick draw, sure. I'm quick as molasses in January," she said caustically.

Daggert smiled broadly for the first time in months. "Molasses runs a lot faster in July," he said as he headed to her horse to get the bullets. *There is something good about that woman in spite of her rough behavior,* he mused to himself, *and I like it.*

Daggert took out the box of bullets and carried them over to Carly. He watched her draw for a few minutes, and he was impressed with the improvement she had made since they had started yesterday. "You've been practicing." He handed her the box of shells. "Load it up."

Carly had no practice loading a pistol so it took her a few minutes to get all six shells in the gun. Daggert had her practice loading before he finally said she was ready to shoot.

"What do you want me to shoot?"

"First of all, shoot at that big rock about thirty feet in front of you."

"That's too easy."

"I'm sure it is, but just see if you can hit it, and then we'll find something else to shoot at."

She took the gun in both hands, brought it up in front of her face, and cocked it. She jerked as she pulled the trigger and missed the rock by a couple of feet. She looked over at Daggert, who was trying hard to keep from laughing.

"Something funny?" she snapped.

"No, ma'am, you'll be okay. You just need more practice. Now take a deep breath and hold the gun steady. I do believe your draw is much smoother today. It could be the gun, as well as all your practice," he hastily added.

She ignored his compliment, aimed the gun again, and fired. She saw the same results: she missed the target again. She was now angry with herself, so she shot four times as quickly as she could, without bringing it up to sight and aim. She hit the target three times out of four.

She looked back at Daggert. "Sometimes you can concentrate too hard," he said. "When it's a quick draw, there's no time to sight the target. You did well that time. Load up again."

She loaded up again, fired all of the shots, and hit the target four out of six times.

Daggert said, "Well, now you're getting the hang of it. Load up and try again."

Carly shot several rounds, and then Daggert picked out a small tree only a few feet away. "See if you can put some slugs in the trunk of that tree."

Carly was getting good at loading the gun, and now she was getting excited about hitting the target. Unfortunately, when she tried to hit the tree, she only hit it three times. She was becoming discouraged.

Not Daggert. "Miss Barton, I think you're a natural. First thing you know, you'll be as good as I am," he said with a smile.

"If that's meant to be funny, it isn't."

"Not meant to be funny. I think you could

become a good gunman, or I guess in your case, gunwoman. Or do you prefer gun lady?"

She shook her head and ignored his intended compliment. "Let's get back to work."

An hour later, she was tired and hurting so much that she could hardly lift the gun from her holster. "That's all I can do today. Let's get back to town," she suggested.

He walked over to her and reached for her right hand. It was red and blistered. "You might want to visit the doctor and get something for your hands."

"I'll be fine by tomorrow," she said.

"You're doing okay with the gun, but there are other things you need to learn."

"What would they be?" she asked.

"Remember at all times to notice everything in your surroundings."

"And just how do I do that?"

"Pay attention to everyone around you and particularly the one or ones you are concentrating on. You know, your live target. Notice the way a person walks, the way he holds himself. Pay particular attention to his eyes. Does he look directly at you, or does his attention stray. Study the man's mood, and not necessarily what he says, but the way he speaks. Is he nervous, or does he think he has you figured?"

"I think I understand that. It certainly makes sense."

"Be ready in all situations such as walking into a building. Make sure you allow your eyes to adjust to your surroundings. If you are outside, make sure you are not looking into the sun. Then concentrate on what you are doing. Don't allow a glint of sun on metal, such as a belt buckle, to distract you. It could be deadly."

"So if I'm facing someone in the afternoon, I should be facing east, with my back to the west."

"I think you're getting the hang of it already."

"Still, all of that sounds difficult."

"Yes, it is difficult. That's why you have to practice."

"I'll work on it," she replied testily and headed for her horse.

CHAPTER 11

Clay Daggert had been drinking for a short time when a young man approached and leaned down to look at him at eye level. "You can't be the great gunman, Clay Daggert," he snarled.

Daggert had chosen the table in the corner so he could drink in peace, but apparently, that was not going to happen. He looked at the man who could not be more than twenty years old. He was an ugly, skinny kid, about five feet, seven inches tall, weighing maybe one hundred thirty pounds. What Daggert noticed most were the two, tied-down, pearl-handled Colts in holsters. The leather and studs on the holsters looked freshly oiled and cleaned. "I can be whoever I want," answered Daggert.

"My name is Brett Yates," said the young man. He waited for a reply, or recognition.

"Is that name supposed to mean something to me?" said Daggert indifferently.

"I'm sure you've heard of me. I'm the gunfighter from Abilene. Killed three men."

"Were they facing you?" Daggert asked sarcastically.

"What the hell are you saying?"

"Never mind, kid. Just go away and let me get drunk."

"No. I wanna know what you're implying."

Daggert turned away, looking toward the bartender. "There are plenty of self-proclaimed gunfighters in and around Abilene. Why aren't you still there?"

" 'Cause I've heard that there was an over-the-hill gunny here named Clay Daggert," replied the young man, his voice rising.

"So you traveled all this way, with your fancy rig on your hips, to shoot me?"

"Oh, you like my guns?" the boy asked with a smirk.

"I didn't say I liked them, just that they're fancy. Then I allowed you were a long ways from Abilene."

"Aw, t'was not that fur from Abilene. Besides, I heard that many years ago you were one of the best. Now though, what I'm seein', I ain't so sure. I'm lookin' at a drunken, broke-down, has-been."

"So, you decided you would try to en-hance your reputation by killing an over-the-hill gunman?"

"That's 'bout the size of it. Are you a'comin', or do I have ta force you?"

"So, how much can you enhance your reputation by killing a broke-down, drunken, has-been?"

"Maybe none, but I'd guess I'll jist git the satisfaction of killin' you."

"Why, you little squirt, you couldn't hold my hat, much less gun me."

"Jist 'cause some purty lady hired you to do her killin' don't mean you're not a drunken has-been." The kid backed up a few steps and dropped his hand to his gun. "Why don't we see jist how good you are?"

"No one has hired me to kill anyone, and I have no reason to draw on you. I only killed when I got paid, and when I chose to. You're worth nothin' to me, so I'd suggest that you just turn around and walk out that door."

"Why'd I do that?" the boy jeered.

"Well, you might live, at least for one more night."

"Daggert, you can't bluff me. I'm not leavin', an' you can't get outta this fight that easy. I'm gonna count to three and draw. You better stand up and draw."

The other men in the saloon moved away

from their tables, out of the line of fire, and waited.

"Yates, if that's your name, I'm holding a gun here under this table, and it's aimed at your belly button. I don't know whether or not you can count to three, but I can tell you one thing . . ."

"An' what would that be?" Yates asked as his mind went from confidence to contemplating Daggert's statement.

"When your countin' reaches two, I'm gonna blow a hole in your gut big enough for my fist to go through."

The young man laughed nervously. "You want me to believe you're holdin' a gun under that table. You ain't bluffin' me."

"Suit yourself. Just start counting and then you'll know if I'm bluffing."

The young man's expression turned from a smile to a frown. He stared at the table, trying to see if Daggert had a gun in his hand, but he was not sure. "S-stand up and take it like a-a man," he stuttered.

"I have no intention of standing up, so you might as well go ahead and make your play."

Brett Yates was now confused. Should he go ahead and count or turn and walk out of the saloon? If Daggert were holding a gun, he would surely be killed; however, if he walked out . . . Well for sure, he would be branded as a coward. He would never be able to live that down. He heard the saloon doors bang open and glanced over his shoulder toward the door. A man with a badge pinned to his chest walked through the door.

"Young man, are you looking for someone?" the marshal called out as he walked over.

This was his out. "Guess my business can wait," replied Yates as he turned and headed for the door.

"Young man," said the marshal as Yates walked by him.

Yates stopped and looked at the marshal.

"You trying to gun someone here in town?" asked the marshal.

"Ain't your business," replied Yates.

The marshal looked the young man up and down, and his eyes returned to his fancy guns. "My name is Marshal Sam Warlock, and I'd suggest that you leave town quickly, before it becomes my business."

"Marshal, I ain't breaking no laws here. I'm jist talking sorta friendly like to Mr. Daggert."

"If you're in town at noon, I'll run you in. You hear me?"

"Yes, sir, Marshal, I hear you," replied Yates. He gave Daggert a challenging look and then left the saloon.

The bartender, Mack, walked over to Daggert's table and set a whiskey glass down in front of him, "On the house."

Daggert brought his hand from under the table and took the drink. Mack looked down at him, hesitated a moment, then smiled. "You bluffed him. You didn't have a gun in your hand."

Daggert put his index finger to his lips, looked up at the bartender, smiled, and said, "Shhh, don't tell anyone."

"Clay, you know the word will get out that you bluffed him and he'll be back," said the marshal.

"Not if you run him out of town," replied Daggert.

"Clay, even though I threatened him, I don't really have any reason to run him out of town."

"Then I'll just have to take my chances."

"When was the last time you pulled a gun on anyone?" asked the marshal.

"It's been a few months or so. You know I haven't been in my own mind for some time now."

"Yes, I know. Your mind has been at the bottom of a whiskey bottle." The marshal laughed.

"Yeah, I made a mistake, and I've been paying for it for quite a while now."

"I understand your situation, but at some point, you need to get past that. You could have a long life ahead of you."

"Not if Brett Yates shoots me down."

For the first time that Daggert could remember, he left the saloon early and went to his room. Not that he was afraid of the young gunman, but he had not faced anyone in several months. Was his gun hand ready? Even more important, was his mind ready?

The next morning he had breakfast at the boarding house and headed to the marshal's office. He wanted to find out if the marshal had been able to encourage the young man to leave town. He got his answer before he reached the office. He turned the corner and came face to face with the kid.

"Well, Daggert, this time you ain't got the marshal to back you up. What you gonna do now?" Yates asked. He had an ugly grin on his face.

"Kid, you could have a long life ahead of you, but you shorten your odds every time you challenge someone with a gun," said Daggert.

"I sure don't have to worry 'bout you. You're afraid of me."

"Kid, I'm afraid of anyone I face with a gun, and you should be too."

"Don't call me kid. My name's Brett, and jist why would you say that?"

"It's just possible you'll find someone faster than you."

"No one is faster than me," Yates replied smugly.

Even though it was early in the day, they were drawing a crowd. That was the last thing Daggert wanted. "Well, if you're determined to die, we might as well get it done."

"That's what I been waitin' to hear." The kid chuckled.

"Your move then," said Daggert.

The young man was fast, but Daggert's bullet hit him in the chest before he could pull his trigger. The gunman clutched his chest, stared at Daggert, dropped his gun, and fell to the ground. The shot brought the marshal out of his office with his gun in hand. He saw the crowd, the dead man, and Daggert. He holstered his gun and hurried over to Daggert.

"What happened?"

Daggert searched the crowd, looking for Carly Barton, but he saw no sign of her. He explained what happened, and the marshal asked one of the men to fetch the under-taker.

"Well, there were plenty of witnesses, so I guess all I need is a written statement from you. You can drop by the office sometime today and we'll wrap it up," said the marshal.

"All right, Sam, I'll be there."

CHAPTER 12

Daggert rode out to the flats for his meeting with Carly. She was already there waiting for him. He slid down from his horse as she waited and watched him.

"Heard you had a little trouble this morning," she said.

"I guess so, if you consider a gunfight with a kid trouble. Anyway, I didn't see you in the crowd. How do you know about the shooting?"

"It's all over town. The over-the-hill gunman makes a comeback," she replied wryly.

"You can be sure that it was not of my doing."

"Mr. Daggert, you're a gunman. What difference does it make who you shoot?"

"I thought we were on a first-name basis."

"Yes, I guess so. Are you going to answer my question?"

"Does it make a difference to you?" he asked curiously.

"No. My main interest is learning how to shoot. Everything else is secondary."

"In that case, I'll tell you. I used my gun for money. Whenever someone wanted a man killed, and they had my fee, I obliged."

"So you only killed for money?"

"Yes, with two exceptions."

"And they would be?"

"I don't kill women, and I don't kill anyone who's unarmed."

"That makes sense."

Carly sat down on a rock and looked at him. "Clay, you appear to be an educated man. How did you become a gunfighter when you could have done lots of other things?"

"That's a long story. You sure you want to hear it?"

"I have plenty of time."

"It'll take away from your practice time," he warned.

"I'll make it up later."

He walked over and sat down beside her on the rock. He pulled a tobacco sack from his shirt pocket, rolled a cigarette, found a match, lit the cigarette, and dropped the dead match on the ground. He took a drag on the cigarette, blew out the smoke, and began.

"I was born in Athens, Ohio. My father

was an attorney, so he sent me to college at The Ohio University to be an attorney. Then things began to fall apart. My older brother had a fight with my father and moved to Saint Louis, Missouri. Not long after that my mother died. That bothered me a great deal, because we were very close."

He hesitated a moment, took another drag on his cigarette, and continued, "I've never told this to anyone. I never wanted anyone to know how I felt."

"I'm sorry about your mother," said Carly.

"Well, a short time later we found out that my brother was ambushed and killed in Saint Louis. My father hired the Pinkerton agency to find the killer." He took another drag on his cigarette and crushed it under his boot.

"I'm not following you. Your father hired detectives while you were in college, and now you're a hired gun?"

"You, lady, are too impatient, just like in learning to shoot a gun."

"Well, I want to find those men that killed my parents before they disappear."

"Carly, you may never find those men, and that might be a good thing. The three of them, or even one, could easily kill you, before you could kill them."

She ignored his comment. "So the Pinkertons found your brother's killer, and he was sent to prison."

Daggert smiled. "No, I left college and contacted Grover Osborne, the lead Pinkerton detective. He agreed to allow me to hang around while he tried to find the killer. I bought a gun and spent those next few weeks practicing with it, with his help. Didn't take long to figure I had a knack with a gun. Well, when the Pinkertons found out who was responsible for murdering my brother, I was with them. Before Osborne could get to him, I tracked the man down and killed him."

"How did you kill him?"

"When I found him at his cabin, I identified myself and told him to come out. He came out shooting, but I was shooting better than he was."

"I guess so. You're still here. Did you go to jail?"

"Yes, I was arrested and spent three days in jail. Fortunately, the law found out the man was wanted for several other crimes and that there was a five hundred dollar bounty on him, dead or alive. They released me and gave me five hundred dollars."

"So you decided that killing people was easier than going to college?" she asked.

"Something like that. I guess I just didn't think I was cut out to be a lawyer. Come on, let's get to practicing."

Carly stood and pulled her gun.

"Wait a minute," said Daggert. "How's your hand?"

"Sore, but it won't stop me from shooting."

He muttered under his breath, "I know. Nothing will keep you from shooting."

"What did you say?"

"Uh, nothing." He walked over to his saddlebags and brought out some empty tin cans. He set six of them down several feet in front of her. "Now let's see if you, and your sore hand, can hit these cans."

She jerked the pistol and emptied it, hitting four out of six of the cans. She looked disgustedly at Daggert, but he assured her that she was doing well. She practiced for over an hour before he called a halt.

"Okay, let's talk. It's good to practice with smaller targets, but when you're shooting at a man, you shoot at the largest target, his chest. Just remember, chest is best."

"I'm going to shoot that big fat bastard right in the gut. I'd prefer to shoot his balls off, if I could hit them."

Daggert, slightly shocked, chuckled. "I understand. However, when a man is gut shot, he knows he is dying. If he's strong, he very well may be able to continue to shoot. It could be the difference between you staying alive or dying. By the way, your other idea, although painful, might be difficult to accomplish."

"I want to inflict pain. I want them to know that I shot them, and I want them to suffer as much as possible before they die," she said passionately.

"I hear you, but again, a shot in the chest is best. Shoot as close to the heart as you can get, so they'll bleed faster and die quicker."

"You don't understand. I want to see them in lots of pain. I'm not just trying to kill them."

Daggert jerked his hat off his head and slammed it against his leg in frustration. "Damn it, missy, I'm trying to save your life. If the first one kills you, you won't get all of your revenge."

"I hear what you're saying, but I don't give a damn about my life, after I get my revenge." She emptied the cartridges from the gun, reloaded, and slipped the gun back into the holster. "Set the cans back up."

"No, we're done for today. Tomorrow I'll get you a life-sized poster, and you can practice shooting at it and hitting the chest."

"Yes, sir," she replied, then drew the gun and emptied it into the cans where they lay on the ground in a ragged circle, hitting all of them.

He smiled at her. "I think you're just about ready. That's pretty good shooting for a woman."

"Forget about the 'for a woman' thing. I'm a gunfighter, or I'm going to be."

He looked her up and down. "In spite of your outfit, it's still difficult for me to forget you're a woman."

She glared at him. "If you're so stuck on me being a woman, maybe you should try being one. I'm sure you wouldn't like it."

He nodded thoughtfully while she reloaded the gun. "So, what is the bad part about being a woman?"

She aimed the gun, fired off two shots, then dropped the gun into her holster, "Men and more men," she replied.

He shook his head. "Miss Barton, you got a bad deal. Yes, a really raw deal, but believe it or not, all men are not out to get you."

She turned and looked at him. "And how would you know? You shoot people for a living. I'm sure you wouldn't be helping me, if you weren't getting paid."

Daggert glared at her for several moments, then turned and walked away. He mounted his horse and rode out without looking back. He heard her calling him, but he ignored her.

CHAPTER 13

Daggert had been sitting in the saloon drinking for several hours. In fact, he did not even know how long he had been there, nor did he know how many drinks he had consumed. The only thing he did know was that his glass was empty again. While he waited for another drink, he took out his tobacco sack and rolled a cigarette, or tried to. He spilled more tobacco on the table than went into his paper. He managed to get the cigarette rolled at the same time the bartender came over and stood in front of him.

"Clay, you haven't been in for the last few nights. I thought maybe you had kicked the habit."

"What habit, Mack?"

"You know what habit. You drink too much."

"You know anythin' 'bout women?" he asked as he picked up his glass and moved to the bar.

"I guess not. I was married once but she left me for another man. Why?"

"I was just askin', 'cause my problems aren't 'bout whiskey."

"Clay, you having woman problems?"

"How could I have woman problems? I don't even know any women."

"You're spending a lot of time with the Barton woman."

He ignored him. "I need 'nother drink."

"You've had enough for tonight. Go on home."

"I want 'nother drink," he snapped.

Mack shook his head, then picked up a bottle and filled Clay's glass. "Is she the problem?"

"She who?" Clay asked.

"The Barton woman. You know. Who we were talking about."

"Mack, you know she's much too young for me. Besides, she's just paying for my services."

"Age doesn't always matter."

"Well, it does in this case," he said and spilled part of his drink as he tried to finish it. "Now, I guess it's time to go." He dropped some coins on the bar and staggered out of the saloon. Mack watched him go, shook his head, and turned back to his other customers.

Daggert managed to get through the saloon door and past the saloon window, holding onto the wall to keep from falling. When he got to the end of the wall, he slumped to the sidewalk and asked himself, "Why do I torture myself like this?" He sat there in the dark and no one paid any attention to him. He rested for a while, then staggered over to the boarding house. There was no one around, so he slowly managed the stairs, almost crawling to reach his room. He pushed the door open, took one long stride, and fell forward on the bed. He did not get up until late the next morning.

Carly knew as soon as she spoke those words to Daggert that she had made a big mistake. The man had spent hour after hour trying to help her get where she wanted to be, and now he probably would not even speak to her again. She stood there thinking. Then she told herself she did not need him. She did not need anyone, especially a man. A moment later, she knew that was not true. Yes, she had become good with the pistol, but she needed to learn a lot more, such as how to track and find those three men. She would have to find Daggert and make amends.

Carly rode back to town but, in spite of her search, she never saw Clay Daggert that afternoon. She hoped she would see him in the dining room for supper, but he did not show. She knew that it was not ladylike to chase after a man, but she walked over to the boarding house where he was staying. When the door opened, she introduced herself to Mrs. Woodley, and the older woman came out on the porch.

"Is Mr. Daggert in?"

"No. I assume he's at the saloon. He left here about an hour ago," said Mrs. Woodley.

"All right, Mrs. Woodley. Thank you. I'd better go."

"Miss Barton, for the last couple of nights he was staying around the boarding house. I'd hoped he was going to slow down on his drinking, but I guess he's at it again."

"Why do you think that?" asked Carly.

"When he left here, he was upset about something. He usually talks to me, but when I asked him what was wrong, he snapped at me and told me he was going to get drunk. Then he told me to mind my own business."

"I'm afraid he's angry at me because of something I said to him. That's probably why he went to the saloon."

"He never mentioned anything about that."

"Well, he shaved and cleaned himself up, and then while we were together I said something he didn't like. Now he's mad."

Mrs. Woodley interrupted her. "Young lady, come in. Have a seat, and let me tell you a story."

Carly walked into the parlor, sat down, and Mrs. Woodley sat down next to her. "Clay Daggert came to Darby about nine months ago. I'm not sure why he chose to stop here, but he did. He was drunk when he got here, and has been drunk most of the time since. He stayed in the hotel when he first arrived, but spent all of his money, so when he was broke, the hotel kicked him out."

"So you took him in."

"No, not then. Part of the time the marshal allowed him to sleep in the jail, and other times he lived on the street, or wherever he could find somewhere to stay."

"So how did he get to your place? Did he find some money?"

"No, it was sometime later. The marshal came by and asked me to allow him to stay here. He even paid the first month's rent."

"The marshal paid his rent? Why would he do that?"

"Friends, I guess. Anyway, I wanted to tell you what he told me one night, when he was especially drunk."

Carly leaned forward, listening hard.

"Clay mentioned a woman named Julie. Just for conversation, I asked him who Julie was. Several times I had tried to ask him questions about his past, and he always told me to mind my own business, but in a nice way. This time was different."

"Julie was his wife?" Carly asked.

"No, someone he met and apparently cared for."

"What happened to her?"

"Well, as his story goes, he was in Abilene, Kansas, when he met Julie. I don't know how long they knew each other, but sounded like they were on their way to a café, and two young gunmen accosted them. Clay was a gunman, but he only used his gun when paid, so he tried to talk them out of it. He thought that the two men were just trying to build a reputation, but later on, he found out they were brothers of a man Clay had killed. Apparently, they were trying to avenge their brother's death."

"Two against one. That doesn't seem fair." The three convicts came unbidden into her mind. Nothing about life was fair anyway, she decided.

"You're right, but initially only the older brother was going to challenge Clay. Anyhow, the man drew first, Clay killed him, but then the other man drew, fired, and missed Clay, but hit the woman. Clay killed the second man too, but Julie died in the street."

"So Clay blamed himself for her death," said Carly.

"Yes, and according to him, he hasn't been sober since," replied Mrs. Woodley.

"Except for the last couple of days," said Carly.

"Yes, except for the last couple of days, and I think that was because of you."

"What do you mean?"

"Just a couple of things he mentioned."

"What things?"

"I've already said too much. Please don't mention any of this to anyone. You seem to be good for him, so I just wanted to let you know what's going on with Clay and why he lives the way he does."

"I won't say anything."

"Well, I've got work to do. Thanks for listening," said Mrs. Woodley.

"So do I, and thanks for telling me," replied Carly.

"Young lady, please take my advice and forget about that nonsense you're planning.

Let the law take care of those awful men."

"How do you know what I'm planning? You know my story?"

"It's all over town. You can't keep something like that a secret."

"It doesn't matter. I'm not trying to hide it. It's my job to take care of those men. My parents were the people they killed."

"Carly's revenge?" asked Mrs. Woodley.

"That's right. Carly's revenge."

"Where are you going? Do you know where those men are?"

"I'm heading for Rock Springs." As an afterthought Carly added, "But don't tell anyone."

"As you wish. Good luck and be careful, but I pray you come to your senses."

"Thanks again, Mrs. Woodley." She left the house and Mrs. Woodley watched her until she was out of sight.

Carly did not want to go back to the saloon to look for Clay, so she decided to wait until the next morning to try to talk to him.

CHAPTER 14

Carly slept late the next day. After breakfast she walked back to Woodley's Boarding House. Clay Daggert was not there. Mrs. Woodley told her that he had left an hour or so before but she did not know where he was going. So Carly walked around town looking for him, then gave up and went back to the hotel. In the afternoon, she saddled Brandy, and rode out to the flats, but he was not there. She spent the next couple of hours practicing by herself, but there was still no sign of Daggert.

On the way back to town, she decided she was going to leave Darby the next morning. The men she was looking for said that they were going to Rock Springs, and that was where she needed to be. It would be nice to say goodbye to Clay, but if she couldn't, she would leave the remainder of his money with Mrs. Woodley. When she got to town, she checked the stagecoach office and found that there was a stage to Rock Springs, leaving at ten o'clock in the morning.

The afternoon dragged on for her as she alternated between sitting in her room and walking around town, but she saw no sign of Daggert. After supper, she went to the boarding house, left Daggert's money with Mrs. Woodley, and then stopped at the general store. She bought a man's hat, a jacket, some cloth, a pair of scissors, needles and thread, and went back to her hotel room.

She stood in front of the mirror, scissors in her hand, staring at her long dark hair for several minutes. Then she carefully began to cut it off. It took her awhile before she got the length right, and cutting the back was difficult. Finally, she put her new hat on her head. With that done, she took off her clothing and folded the cloth that she had purchased, creating a binder. She wrapped the binder around her breasts, flattening them enough so that when worn beneath her loose-fitting shirt, no one could tell she was a woman. Fortunately for her, her breasts were not very big. When she got her breasts as flat as she wanted, she cut the cloth and sewed the ends together. She put the binder on, then the shirt, and then the jacket she had purchased, and looked in the mirror. She was satisfied that she could pass as a young man if she could deepen her voice. She would have to practice a new voice.

Early the next morning Carly avoided the dining room, went to the kitchen, asked the cook for some biscuits, and drank a cup of coffee. Back in her room, she packed her meager belongings, strapped on her gun and holster, came downstairs, and left the key at the desk. The desk clerk stared at her but did not speak. She ignored him and left the hotel. She stopped at the livery stable and sold Brandy for forty dollars. Pap O'Dell agreed to sell the mare back to her if she came back this way anytime soon. She carried her belongings to the stage office, purchased a ticket, and waited for the stage to come in.

The stage arrived late, but Carly did not mind. When the stage left town, it held two male passengers and Carly. She was sure that one of the men was a professional gambler, while the other looked like a rancher. She did not speak to either of the men until some time had passed and the man with the fancy clothing asked her, "Young man, do you play cards?"

Carly braced herself against the rocking motion of the coach. "Never played," she replied nervously in her new voice. Apparently, she did not give herself away because neither of the men looked surprised.

"Would you like to learn? Something to pass the time, since we have several more hours on this stage."

"Difficult to play cards in a coach," she said, keeping her words to a minimum.

"Guess you haven't ridden a stagecoach very often."

She remembered the trip west, when she walked until her feet were so sore she could not walk anymore, and then she was allowed to ride on the wagon, for a while at least. "No."

"You'll get used to it, and the game may take your mind off the rough ride," he said with a smile.

She started to say no but then changed her mind. Knowing how to play cards could come in handy. Clay was going to teach her but she did not know where he was now, or if she would ever see him again. "I don't have much money."

"That's okay. We'll just play for fun, at least in the beginning."

"You a professional gambler?" asked the other man.

"Yep, gambled from New Orleans, to Mississippi riverboats, and as far west as Dodge

City," he answered proudly.

"You always win?" asked Carly.

"Young man, nobody always wins, but I win on a regular basis. By the way, my name is Ned Miller."

Carly started to give her real name but caught herself. "Carl. Carl Barton."

"Carl, you look pretty young. You live around here?" asked the other man.

"Nope, just passing through."

"I'm Clint Adams," said the man who looked like a rancher, and he extended his hand. Carly was wary about her hands looking feminine, but the older man did not appear to notice.

The gambler pulled out a deck of cards and began to shuffle them. "Do you know anything about cards?"

Carly's parents did not approve of gambling, so she never had a chance to play with cards but she had heard about them. She knew about the suits and face cards but that was just about it. "Very little."

The gambler stopped shuffling and handed the deck over to her. "See if you can shuffle."

She had watched him shuffle, but when she tried, the cards flew in the air. The two men helped her pick them up. The gambler took back the cards and slowly demonstrated how to shuffle. After several tries, Carly was able to shuffle the cards without dropping them. Even though the stagecoach ride was rough, they were able to play. Ned not only instructed, but also offered several tips. The last few hands were played for money, and she was able to come out ahead by a few dollars. She figured the two men had allowed her to win, but she did not care. She needed the money, and she was not going to complain.

"You're a natural card shark," said the gambler.

"Must be luck. As I said before, I've never played cards."

"Well, in order to be a good player, you need a lot of luck," said Clint.

"And you don't have luck?" asked Ned.

"Absolutely not with cards. That's why I don't play very often. Lady Luck doesn't shine on me," replied Clint with a grin.

"You have to be willing to take some losses because everyone does, professional or amateur."

"Do you cheat?" asked Carly.

The gambler looked at Carly with a wry smile. "Young man, asking a gambler a question like that could get you killed."

"Yes, especially if there is money on the table," added the rancher.

"Just a lesson learned," said the gambler.

"I guess I need to learn a lot, and a lot sooner than later," said Carly.

The rancher looked at Carly and down at the gun she wore on her hip, "You any good with that pistol?"

"I'm good enough."

"A little cocky, aren't you?" asked the gambler.

"You're a gambler. I assume you expect to win money when you play because you are good. I would say that's cocky. I'm good with this gun, and you can call it whatever you like."

"When I hire cowhands, I want them to be good and somewhat cocky," said the rancher.

"I suppose you're right," answered the gambler.

The stagecoach rolled to a stop. "Everybody out to stretch your legs," yelled the driver.

The gambler looked at his watch. "We've been on the road over four hours. Time went by quickly."

The rancher got out, followed by Ned, leaving Carly to step down last. She was startled for a moment, then realized they really did think she was a man, and folks were not going to wait for her, or help her down. When she stepped down, she adjusted the gun on her hip and headed for the relay station.

There was food on the table, and she wasted no time digging in. "Eat hearty. You have five hours before we get to Bakers Crossing," said the driver.

About thirty minutes later, the stage rolled out of the relay station heading west. "Mr. Barton, where are you heading, if you don't mind my asking?" asked the rancher.

"Rock Springs, looking for some acquaintances of mine."

"I have a ranch just a few miles out of Rock Springs. Who are they? I may know of them."

Carly gave the names and descriptions of the three men, but did not tell him how she had met them. "Ever seen any of them?"

The rancher rubbed his mustache with his right hand, thinking about it, and then studied her before answering. "There were two men who came by the ranch, and kind of fit your descriptions, looking for jobs."

"Did you hire them?" she asked.

"Hell, no. I didn't like the way they looked, acted, or talked, so I just sent them packing. I do understand that they went to work for the Lazy L."

"Where's the Lazy L?"

"A couple miles west of my spread. Judging by their looks, I wouldn't think they were friends of yours."

"I'm sure Carl can take care of himself," said the gambler with a knowing look at Carly's holstered gun.

"Well, young men often get in trouble because of who they run with," said the rancher.

She didn't want to be lectured to, so Carly ignored the two men and tried to sleep. However, the creaking noises and the rocking and swaying of the stage made it difficult. She dozed, and was aware of the two men's conversation, but she no longer cared what they were saying.

CHAPTER 15

Carly was relieved when the stage finally rolled into Bakers Crossing. It stopped in front of the Baker Hotel and she stepped down as soon as it came to a stop. Even though her legs were not that long, they still cramped up after riding those several hours in the stage. The driver dropped the luggage, and she picked hers up and headed for the hotel door. As she walked, she remembered to take longer strides so as not to show any feminine traits. The man at the desk gave her a key and she started for the stairs.

"Mr. Barton, how about supper in the dining room?" asked the rancher. Carly hesitated for a moment, then agreed. "How about in thirty minutes and after that we can go get a drink?" he added.

She was a little concerned about the drinking part, but she might as well face it: she would have to visit saloons. The men she longed to kill loved saloons, and that was how she could find them. "I'll meet you in the dining room in thirty minutes," she answered and went upstairs.

She dropped her hat and luggage on the bed, picked up the water pitcher, and poured some water in the bowl. She washed her hands and face, unbuckled her gun belt, let it slide to the floor, and then she fell onto the bed. She had planned to rest a few minutes but she fell asleep. She came awake when there was loud knocking on her door. She opened the door and the rancher was standing there.

"Son, you must be a heavy sleeper. I've knocked several times."

"Sorry," she said. "I haven't had much sleep lately."

"No problem. Let's get downstairs for some grub."

"I can go for that." Carly picked up her hat, put it on, and strapped on her gun belt. "I'm ready." She followed the rancher downstairs to the dining room. While they were eating, they chatted.

"Carl, if you're looking for a job, I can always use a good hand at the ranch," offered the rancher.

"Thanks for the offer, Mr. Adams, but I'm not much good as a cowhand. Besides, I have something to take care of before I'm tied down to a steady job."

"Call me Clint, and you just let me know when you're ready. Keep in mind that no cowhand was any good before he started. I own the Bar C Ranch. Anyone around Rock Springs can give you directions."

"I guess you're right, Clint. I'll keep your offer in mind, and thanks."

They finished eating and headed for the saloon. Bakers Crossing was rather small, so it only had the one saloon, named Trail's End. They walked up to the bar and Carly waited for the rancher to order. He ordered whiskey and when it came, he told the bartender to leave the bottle and bring two glasses.

"Clint, I'm not used to drinking," she said, as she remembered her first drink of brandy Mr. Johnson had given her.

"That's what I figured. Just sip it slowly, and no one will be any the wiser," he replied with a broad grin.

Carly took one sip of the drink, and she could feel it burning all the way down her throat. She made a face and the rancher smiled again. "Don't let anyone see your expression. They'll think you're a tender-foot."

"Just between you and me, I am a tenderfoot, at least when it comes to whiskey."

"You can be a tenderfoot, as long as you don't act like one."

She sipped the whiskey again. It still burned, but this time it went down a little easier. She still did not like it.

"I think you're getting the hang of it now," said Clint.

"I don't know. It'll probably take much more than two drinks to get the hang of it," she replied with a weak grin.

The rancher laughed. "Carl, I see our gambler friend, Ned, over at that table and there's an empty chair."

"Go right ahead. I'll just stand here and slowly sip my drink."

Adams picked up the bottle, poured some whiskey in her glass, and set the bottle back down. "That should hold you for a while and I'll be back. Try not to act like a tenderfoot." He chuckled.

She took another small sip and watched the rancher walk away. The table was quite far away, and the crowd noise kept her from hearing any conversations. Adams spoke to the gambler, then sat down in the empty chair. She continued to lean on the bar, watching the customers, not wanting to miss anything in case the men she was looking for walked in. A short squat cowboy came through the door. He looked around, then headed directly toward her. She did not know the man so she just stood and watched him.

He moved in close to her, bumping her shoulder, as he ordered whiskey. There was plenty of room at the bar, so she knew he bumped her intentionally, but she ignored him, moved away, and turned to hunch over the bar.

"Leave the bottle," said the cowboy loudly.

Carly got the impression he was already drunk, but then again, she did not really know much about drunks, unless they were staggering around. The cowboy quickly downed the drink, poured another, and then looked at Carly. "Boy, ain't you a little young to be drinkin' and carryin' that pistol?"

Carly ignored the man and stared ahead. She was hoping he would get the hint and leave her alone but her luck was out. He poked her shoulder with a finger. "Boy, I'm talking to you," he snarled.

She remembered her pledge that she was not going to take any guff from any man. Without looking at him she snapped, "Mister, you are a drunken lout, and don't call me boy. And yes, I heard you and so did everyone else here."

"Are you saying I'm a loudmouth?"

"You said it, not me."

He backed away a couple of steps. "Boy, you got a gun. You better get ready to use it."

Carly's anger flared as her mind flashed back to the day her parents were killed. With one sudden move, her right hand went down and came up with the gun pointing at the cowboy's chest, before he knew what happened. However, before she could fire, she felt a big hand on her wrist. "Don't do it, he's not worth it."

Her eyes focused on the speaker. It was Clint Adams. "Leave me alone," she said. "He started it, and I'm going to finish it."

"I'm sorry," the cowboy shouted. "I didn't know you were a gunman. I don't wanna die here."

"Carl, just let it go. He apologized," added Ned the gambler, standing behind Clint.

She hesitated for several moments, "Okay. I'll let him go, this time."

The rancher let go of her hand and she dropped the revolver back into the holster. The cowboy dropped some coins on the bar and hurried out of the saloon.

The rancher put his hand on her shoulder. "Why don't we sit at that empty table and talk?"

"All right," she said, realizing she was a bit shaky.

Carly and the rancher walked over to the table and sat. Ned joined them. The bartender brought the bottle from the bar and three glasses.

The gambler poured drinks and then spoke to Carly. "Young man, I've been around a long time, but I haven't seen a faster draw than yours since Ben Thompson in Abilene, Kansas."

"I've heard a lot about Thompson. Many say he's the fastest gun ever," said the rancher. "Of course, many believe that Billy the Kid is faster."

"I don't know about the Kid, but I've seen Thompson, and I certainly wouldn't bet against him. Some say he's so quick that he could sneak daylight past a rooster. Then again, the Kid is probably not much older than you are," said the gambler, looking at Carly.

"I don't think the Kid is even twenty years old," said the rancher, "and Thompson is an experienced gun hand."

"Not sure if anyone even knows exactly how old the Kid is," said the gambler.

"How did you meet Thompson?" asked the rancher.

"Well, he's also quite a gambler, and that's

how I met him."

"You lose money to him?" asked Carly.

"Let me put it this way. Yes! I was in Abilene when he first rode in, supposedly with only enough money to buy a meal and a room. He pawned his six-gun for a few dollars and came in the saloon on Texas Street where I was playing. Before he quit that night, he had won more than twenty-five hundred dollars."

"You were in the game?" she asked.

"Damn right, and I lost my shirt. So did several other men. Later on, Thompson opened the Bull's Head Saloon with another gunman named Phil Coe. No doubt, some of the money he spent opening that saloon came out of my pocket."

The rancher looked over at Carly. "How did you learn to draw like that?"

"I had a good teacher."

"And who would that be, if you don't mind telling?" asked the gambler.

"Clay Daggert."

"Daggert, yes. He was quite a gunfighter. He sort of dropped out of sight. Where did you run into him?"

"Darby, but he was drunk most of the time, so it would be easy to miss him."

"Too bad. I hear he also was quite a gambler."

"He told me he was going to teach me to play cards one day, but we never got 'round to it."

"Well, Carl, I've heard enough stories for one night. I'm going to head back to the hotel. You want to tag along, or do you want to shoot someone?" the rancher asked with a chuckle.

"Sure I'll tag along. I don't see anyone here that I want to shoot anyway," she said sheepishly.

"And I'm going to see if I can win some money before I turn in," said Ned.

"Good luck," said the rancher. He and Carly left the saloon and headed for the hotel. Reaching her hotel room, Carly wasted no time getting to bed. In spite of her nightmares, she slept better than she had in several nights.

CHAPTER 16

The next morning Carly ate breakfast and carried her luggage to the stage. Clint Adams was already there. She asked about Ned, and the driver said he had decided to stay on for a while. During the boarding, a woman and a child bought tickets and joined them. Carly was not sure how old the woman was, but she guessed that the boy was about nine or ten.

There was not much conversation from Carly. She nodded off several times and listened the few times the others spoke. The boy asked Carly if she was a gunfighter and his mother quickly scolded him.

"Just curiosity. The boy will need to learn a lot of things if he stays around here," said the rancher.

"My Timmy's much too young to learn about guns or gunfighters," Timmy's mother replied.

"I'm almost eleven," said the boy indignantly.

"You just turned ten, and even if you were eleven, you would still be too young."

"Aw, Mom, I don't ever —"

She interrupted, "Don't you 'Aw, Mom' me! Just listen to me and stay away from guns."

"Ma'am, I'm Clint Adams. I own a ranch outside of Rock Springs."

"I'm Sarah McNally, and this is my son, Timmy."

"Glad to meet you Mrs. McNally, and you too, Timmy."

Carly turned to look out of the window, and watched the countryside go by. She thought about her younger brother. He would be about this boy's age if he had not died three years ago. If he were alive, her parents would also be alive, and they would all be living back east. Her father thought a change of scenery would be good for her mother, so they had packed up and headed west. Her thoughts slipped away and she soon dozed off. She did not wake up until they reached a way station.

The rancher stepped down first, then helped the woman down. Carly waited for the boy to jump down, and then she stepped down. The woman and the rancher walked together to the house, and the boy walked beside Carly, watching her closely. "Have you ever killed anyone?" he asked quietly, so his mother could not hear him.

"No, Timmy. I've never killed anyone, at least not yet."

"Are you going to?" he asked excitedly.

Before Carly could answer, the woman turned and hollered at the boy. "Timmy, come on and leave the man alone."

"Ah, Mom, I can't do nothin'."

"Timmy." Timmy's mother spoke to the boy sharply.

"Yes, ma'am," he answered, still looking at Carly. The boy continued to look at Carly, shuffling his feet, until his mother looked back at him again, and then he ran ahead to the house. The boy sat across the table from Carly and stared at her the entire time. She was beginning to wonder if he thought she was a woman in disguise, but then decided she did not give a damn if he did.

When they loaded back into the stage, Carly concentrated on the scenery and tried to nap some. Soon the boy changed his attention from Carly to the rancher, Clint.

"What do you do, mister?" the boy asked.

"Timmy," scolded the boy's mother, "leave the man alone."

"I don't mind, ma'am. Let the boy talk," the rancher said.

The boy became quite fascinated when the rancher began talking about his ranch, the cows, horses, and the cowboys. He was especially interested in hearing about the horses.

"I'm going to have my own horse someday, mister," said the boy.

His mother frowned. "Timmy, his name is Mr. Adams, and it will be quite a few years before you get a horse."

"Mr. . . . uh, Mr. Adams, when did you get your first horse?" he asked, trying to keep the enthusiasm from his voice.

"Well, son, I rode my first horse when I was five, but like your mother, my mother didn't like me riding that young either."

"So then how did you get to do it?"

"My father wanted me to learn how to ride young. Not only ride, but do a lot of other things around the ranch, because he needed help and couldn't afford to hire anyone."

"That's much too early for a boy to have to work," Mrs. McNally said.

The rancher looked over at her. "Do you mind if I ask you a question?"

"Of course not," she replied.

"Where are you from?"

"We're from Pittsburgh, Pennsylvania."

"I've never been to Pittsburgh but I've been to Saint Louis, and I guess it's about the same. Out here, life is very different. Everyone has a job, young or old, and no one gets to skip out."

"What about schooling? That's so important."

"Aw, Mom, I hate school," Timmy interrupted.

Before Mrs. McNally could reprimand him, Clint broke in. "Son, I went to school. I can read, write, and do arithmetic. I have to, in order to run the ranch. School is important. I went to school, and still did all my chores at the ranch."

"That's too much for a little boy," Mrs. McNally said. "My husband didn't have any education. He was killed in a factory accident, working twelve hours a day. His life was worth two hundred dollars. That's what the company gave me, and then they kicked us out of company housing."

"I'm sorry," said the rancher.

"I am too," she answered bitterly. Timmy became very quiet and looked out the window.

"You have folks in the area?" Clint asked.

"My husband has an uncle in Colorado, and he has agreed to let us live with him.

We moved to Portsmouth, Ohio, to live with his parents, but after a few months, they decided we were too much trouble."

"Mrs. McNally, how would you and Timmy like to visit my ranch? It's not much out of your way. I have plenty of room, and you could leave whenever you like."

"We couldn't impose on you like that."

"Yes, we could, Mommy! I want to visit a ranch," said Timmy.

"Mrs. McNally, it will not be a bother, and it might be good for Timmy."

Mrs. McNally thought about it for a moment. She was worried about their reception in Colorado, and it would be nice to delay that. "Please, Mommy," the boy pleaded.

She looked at the rancher, "All right, under two conditions."

"Sure. What are they?"

"If it's all right with your wife, and that you will call me Sarah."

"Sarah it is, and I don't have a wife," replied the rancher.

"Oh, I'm sorry," said Mrs. McNally. "Maybe I could do the cooking."

"I have a cook, but I'm sure he won't mind some help," replied Clint.

"Yippee! Oh, boy, I get to ride a horse," exclaimed Timmy.

"Hold your horses, Timmy. We'll see, but only with your mother's permission," said the rancher.

"Yes, Timmy, and now I want you to leave Mr. Adams alone. I'm sure he has other things to think about," said Mrs. McNally. Now she was worried about what it would look like for her to stay at the rancher's home as neither of them were married. In her mind, she reviewed her finances to see if a night at the hotel was possible.

The conversation ended, and Carly listened to the clinking of the horses' harness and the driver yelling to urge them on. She was sore from the bumpy road, and the dust coming in the window made her eyes red and watery. She could not nap, and she was bored by the unending prairie, so she decided to try to find out more about the men she was after.

"Clint, I need to know more about the town of Rock Springs and the people living there. You told me earlier that you believe two of the men I'm looking for might be there."

"Well, there's a marshal in Rock Springs, and he's quite good at his job. I'm sure he would be happy to help you," replied the rancher.

"I doubt the marshal would be happy to

help me."

"Then you're planning to do something that wouldn't have the marshal's approval?" he asked.

"Could say that. I have a job to do, and I'm the only one to do it."

"I see. Well, I'll be glad to give you as much information as I can, but I would suggest you be extremely careful. If you're after the two men I saw, you wouldn't want to tangle with them."

"Thanks for the warning. I'll surely try to be careful."

He continued the conversation, telling her about the town, the marshal, and the surrounding ranches. Carly felt sure that at least two of the men she was looking for were still in or around Rock Springs. She was getting anxious to get there and find those men.

CHAPTER 17

Clay Daggert reined in and dismounted in front of the Woodley Boarding House. He climbed the stairs, opened the door, and met Mrs. Woodley coming from the kitchen.

"Clay, where have you been?"

"I had to run an errand for the marshal," he replied. "I didn't know anyone would miss me."

"Well, that young lady must have missed you. In fact, she told me to say goodbye to you, and then she left town."

"Carly?" he asked.

"How many young women do you know? Of course, it was Carly."

"Where did she go?"

"Don't know," Mrs. Woodley answered, and handed him some money.

"What's this for?"

"She said this was the money she owed you. Of course, I took out what you owe me."

"Oh, uh, of course, Mrs. Woodley. You sure she didn't say where she was going?"

"I promised not to tell you, but I'm worried she's going to get herself killed."

"I'm not so sure. She's better than good with a gun."

"But still, she's just a woman, even in that get-up. Go after her. She asked me not to tell you, but she's heading to Rock Springs."

"Better not tell her that she's 'just a woman,' " he warned her. "I have to take care of my horse and change clothes. How 'bout fixing me some grub to take along? Rock Springs is a fur piece."

"So you're going to follow her?"

"Nothing better to do," he answered.

"I'll fix some food, and it'll be ready in an hour."

"Much obliged, Mrs. Woodley. Did she say she was riding her horse to Rock Springs?"

"I'm sorry, she didn't say. Would she be able to stay on the trail by herself?"

Clay did not look back as he left, thinking Mrs. Woodley was a smart woman. Her question had answered his question.

Clay took his horse to the livery stable and asked Pap O'Dell to take care of him. "Did Miss Barton check her horse out?" he asked. He was quite sure the answer would be no.

"Mr. Daggert, she sold her horse to me yesterday and said she was leaving town."

"So she left on the stage?"

"Don't know any other way."

"Thanks, Pap. Say, can you loan me a good horse, and keep mine until I get back?"

"Shore. When do you want it?"

"About an hour."

"I've got a long-legged dun that'll take you anywhere you wanna go. I'll have it saddled and ready for you then."

"Thanks again, Pap."

Daggert walked down the street to the marshal's office and explained what he was planning to do. In spite of the marshal's objections, Daggert decided to continue.

"Well, since you won't take my advice, I'd suggest you ride through Bakers Crossing. She might have gotten off the stage there."

"Much obliged, Sam. I'll take that advice." Daggert waved and headed for the boarding house.

After he ate the meal Mrs. Woodley had prepared for him, he walked to the livery stable. Pap was waiting with the dun horse. "Doesn't look like much, but he's a fine animal," said Pap.

Clay looked the horse over. "Certainly

looks like a durable animal. Thanks again, Pap. I'll see you, hopefully, in a few days."

"I'm not worried about the horse. The one you're leaving is as good as the one you got there."

Clay led the horse down the street to the general store so he could stock up, especially tobacco and coffee. Within his allotted hour, he was well on the road toward Bakers Crossing.

The dun appeared to be a good choice of horseflesh. Clay kept him at a steady gallop, and he ran without faltering. About two hours later, Daggert came to a watering hole, reined in, and dismounted. The dun drank and grazed while Daggert ate some of the food that Mrs. Woodley had prepared for him. After he was finished, he built a smoke, took a few drags, and mounted up. He was hoping to make Bakers Crossing before dark.

CHAPTER 18

Carly walked into the Red Lilly Saloon in Rock Springs, looked around, and her eyes fixed on five men playing cards at a corner table. She glanced away, then looked back. One of the men looked familiar. He had grown a beard and his hair was longer, but she would recognize him anywhere. Rod Ulrich, killer. Apparently, he was trying to change his appearance, but that did not fool her. She scanned the room for the other two killers as she headed for the bar.

The rancher had suggested she try beer, since the whiskey was not to her liking, so she ordered a beer, sipped it, and watched the table.

"You must be a stranger around these parts," said the bartender.

Startled, she turned toward the man. "Just got in yesterday, name's Barton."

"Glad to meet you, Mr. Barton. You gamble?"

"I play some," she replied with her deepest voice.

"I'm sure those men won't mind you sitting in for a few hands."

"Thanks. I may try later."

"Well, Barton, if you want to get in, I'll talk to them. You need another beer?"

"No thanks, on both accounts." The bartender started to turn away and Carly asked him, "Do you know all of the men playing?"

"Sure. Four of the men are regulars." He pointed at the man Carly knew as Rod. "The fifth man there, Elmer . . . Elmer Trace, has only been around town a few days. Says he works on one of the local ranches."

"He looks familiar. You know anything about him?" she asked.

"Can't say that I do. The only time he speaks to me is when he wants rye whiskey."

"Thanks anyway. I'm probably mistaken about knowing him."

The bartender walked down the bar to another customer, and Carly stood there sipping her beer and studying the man the bartender identified as Elmer Trace. He could call himself whatever he wanted to, she thought, but she knew he was the Rod Ulrich who killed her folks and raped her.

After a few minutes, she picked up her beer and walked over to the table where the five men were playing.

"This seat taken?" she asked and sat down before anyone could answer.

All of them looked up, and one asked, "How old are you, Sonny?"

"I'm old enough," she said dryly. "And don't call me Sonny."

"I don't care how old he is. We need some new blood in here. I haven't won a damn hand in nigh on thurty minutes," snarled the man sitting next to Elmer.

"Playing table stakes," said the first man to speak. "Just put your money on the table. My name's Jess, these other gents are Trey, Josh, Tiny, and Elmer."

Carly pulled out some money and laid it on the table. She nodded at each of the men. "Name's Carl."

"Glad to meet you," said Jess.

"Forget the greetings. Let's play," said the man named Josh.

Trey dealt the cards. Carly got a queen high and folded. It took her five hands before she won with three sevens. Each time she glanced at Elmer, he was staring at her.

"Something wrong?" she asked.

"Oh no, jist thought maybe I've seen you before," he answered.

"And where would you know me from?"

He frowned and dropped his gaze to his cards. "Guess I was mistaken."

"Forget it and play cards," said Josh.

Carly ignored Josh. "Tell me where you're from, and maybe I can help you remember." She wondered what Elmer would say, but he did not answer.

They played a few more hands. "I'm looking for a job," she said. "Anyone know any ranches hiring?" She did not really want a job, but she wanted to find out where these men worked, especially Elmer. Unfortunately, Elmer was not talking, and Josh only wanted to play cards. She played a few more hands, and won a couple, so she was about four dollars ahead before she cashed in. She went back to the bar and ordered another beer.

She slowly drank the beer and waited for Elmer to leave. It was a weekday evening, and she knew ranch hands seldom came into town unless they were on an errand. Elmer seemed in no hurry to get back to the ranch. That fact alone convinced her that he was not running an errand in town. It was almost ten o'clock when he cashed in his chips, finished his beer, and left the saloon.

Carly dropped some coins on the bar to

cover her drinks and followed him out of the saloon. She waited until he mounted his horse and rode out. She mounted the lanky bay horse she had rented from the livery stable and followed him out of town. It was dark, but there was enough light from the moon to keep the man in sight. He was not in a hurry, and apparently, he had no idea anyone would follow him, so she had no problem keeping him in sight. *He is so careless, I'm surprised he hasn't been caught by someone,* she mused.

At one point, the road curved. As she started around the curve, she saw his horse drinking from a stream, and Rod Ulrich still in the saddle. She quickly jerked on the reins of her horse to stop before he saw her, but the horse neighed in protest. Carly slid down from the horse and put her hand on his mouth to keep him quiet.

"Who's out there?" Ulrich yelled.

Carly tightened her hand on the horse's mouth, hoping he would not give her away. She stood there quietly and watched the man roll and light a cigarette. When he struck the match, she could see that he was looking down the road in her direction, but she was sure he could not see her. She did not want to spook him yet, so she needed to stay farther back and keep alert. After what seemed to be an eternity, he flipped the cigarette away, spurred his horse quickly, and rode on at a faster pace than before.

Carly had her rifle in the scabbard. She was certain she could knock the man off his horse, but that was not what she wanted. He was not going to die that easy, or that quick. He was going to know who shot him, and he was going to die slowly.

After a few miles, Ulrich left the main road, angling northwest. Carly stopped at the intersection before following and saw a sign. She had to ride close to read it in the dark, "Lazy L Ranch One Mile." She dug her heels in the bay's flanks and slowly continued toward the Lazy L. Several minutes later, she rode to a gully, stopped to be sure no one was hiding or waiting for her, then went up onto a small hill. She reined in and saw lights from what she decided were the ranch house and the bunkhouse. Ulrich had dismounted and was leading his horse toward the corral. She stayed just below the rise, so he would not see her. She looked around but could not see much. It looked like the hill behind the bunkhouse was higher than the hill on which she stood. She decided that when it was light, she would climb that hill to survey the ranch. She turned the horse around and headed back to town. She gave the horse his head, and about thirty minutes later, she was at the outskirts of Rock Springs.

She returned the horse to the livery stable. There was no sign of the proprietor, so she slipped the saddle and bridle off the horse, then let him walk into a stall. She walked over to a pile of hay, picked up an armload, and carried it to the stall. The water bucket was half-full, so when the horse started munching on the hay, Carly picked up her rifle and headed for the hotel.

The old man at the desk was sleeping in his chair. It took Carly a couple of tries to awaken him.

"Young man, don't you know what time it is?" he asked gruffly.

"I'd say around midnight."

"People your age should be in bed before midnight," he said as he picked up the key to her room and handed it to her.

She was going to tell him to go to hell but decided not to. Instead, she took the key and climbed the stairs to her room. Within a few minutes, she was in bed and sleeping.

CHAPTER 19

The first person Carly saw when she walked into the dining room the next morning was the marshal, who was on his way out. She had not met him before, but when she sat down at a table, he walked over.

"Stranger in town, I see. I'm Marshal Joe Shipman," he said.

Carly looked up at the marshal. He was a strapping man of about fifty, with a barrel chest. He stood over six feet tall, and had large hands. "I'm Carl Barton."

"You have business in town?" he asked.

"My own," she snapped back. "Is it a crime to be new in town?"

The marshal, taken aback by her anger, retorted, "Not unless you're wanted by the law."

"Marshal, I can assure you that I am not wanted, by anyone, anywhere."

Shipman shook his head. "Anything I can do, let me know," he said and left the room.

The waitress came over, and Carly ordered coffee and breakfast. Carly thought maybe she'd been too hard on the marshal; after all, he was just doing his job. Then again, she did not want him to get into her business.

She finished breakfast and headed to the livery stable. She needed to rent a horse and ride out to the Bar C Ranch. Clint Adams had promised to sell her a horse. She rented the horse, received directions from the man at the stable, and headed out to the Bar C. She reached the ranch without meeting anyone on the road, and she was thankful for that.

She rode into the yard and reined in. She stayed in the saddle until the rancher came out. "Mr. Barton, good to see you again. Get down and stretch your legs."

"Thanks," she said as she dismounted.

"You decided to take up my offer of a job?"

"No, not really. I need a horse, and you told me on the stage that you would be willing to sell me one."

"Sure, glad to. Come on. Let's go down to the corral."

Carly followed the rancher to the corral, and they looked out over the twenty or so horses. As the two were discussing the horses, another man joined them.

"Barton, let me introduce you to my foreman, Dave Slaughter. Dave, this is Carl Barton."

They shook hands and Adams explained that Carl was looking for a horse. "That buckskin over there would be a good ride for you," said the foreman.

"Isn't he a little spirited?" asked the rancher.

"Yes, but he has staying power, and I don't think this young man will have a problem riding him," said the foreman. "I'll catch him for you and you can see for yourself." He took a rope from the fence and walked into the corral. The buckskin shied away from the foreman, but after a few minutes, Slaughter caught the horse, and brought it back to where Carly and Adams were standing.

Carly walked around the horse, examining him. Finally, she looked at the two men. "I say around seven years old and in good shape."

"You're a good judge of horseflesh," said the rancher. "Will the buckskin fill your needs?"

"Yes, he will do nicely. How much are you asking for him?"

The rancher glanced at the foreman.

"What do you think? About fifty dollars including saddle and bridle?"

"Boss, I think the horse would be a steal for that price."

"That price certainly suits me," said Carly.

"Then fifty dollars it is," said the rancher with a smile. "Dave, find a saddle and throw it on Boney." He turned back to Carly. "You need time to raise the money?"

"No, I have the money." She pulled out her money sack, counted out fifty dollars, and handed it to the rancher. "His name is Boney?"

"Yes, but that's a long story. Feel free to change his name."

"No, it's unusual, but I like it. I think I'll keep his name. What's the short version?"

"About the name?" he asked.

"Yes, Boney."

"The mare, Bone's mother, died during his birth. For a while, it was touch and go whether the colt would survive. We tried getting him with another mare but that didn't work, so we hand-fed him."

"That must've worked out well."

"Eventually, but for a long time all I remembered were those skinny legs trying to keep him upright. That's why we called him Boney, and that's the end of the story. Anything else I can do for you?"

"No, I think that will be all. Thanks for your help, and thanks for the story."

"Now Carl, if you need a job, don't hesitate to let me know."

"I will. Say, have you arranged a visit for Sally and Timmy McNally?"

"Actually, they are here now. They came out yesterday afternoon. She's a wonderful cook." Clint Adams smiled.

"You invited them out so she could cook for you?" she asked incredulously.

"Of course not. She insisted she wanted to cook a meal for us. She's low on funds, so I've hired her to stay and cook for a few days."

"And all the men are grateful for a change in cooking," added the foreman with a chuckle.

"You want to walk up to the house and visit them?" asked Adams.

"No thanks, Clint. I've got a lot to do."

"Good luck, and come back any time."

The foreman held the horse while Carly mounted. The buckskin pranced and threw up his head, but Carly tightened the reins and kept him in control. Then the foreman handed her the reins of the rented horse and Carly headed back to town, trailing the rented horse.

CHAPTER 20

Carly reached town, returned the rented horse to the livery stable, transferred her saddlebags to the buckskin, and headed for the café. She tied Boney at the hitch rail and went inside. When she finished eating, she mounted and headed for the Lazy L Ranch. About forty-five minutes later, she reached her destination. She left the main road and circled around to the big hill that overlooked the ranch. She tied the buckskin to a tree that was out of sight of the ranch and took out her father's field glasses. She walked on up the hill, found a spot where she could observe what was going on, and sat down. She leaned against a tree and trained the glasses on the ranch house and the bunkhouse.

She saw a few men coming and going, but she did not recognize any of them as the men she was looking for. After sitting for a couple of hours, she gave up for the day and headed back to town. She went to the saloon and ordered a beer. There were only five men in the room, and they were playing cards. Carly did not recognize any of them so she asked the bartender, "Any of those men from the Lazy L Ranch?"

"Yes, the one with his back to us. Why?"

"Just curious, I guess."

"You know, young man, most of the men at the Lazy L are wanted by the law for one reason or another."

"So if they are wanted by the law, why doesn't the marshal arrest them?"

"They may not be wanted in this territory, or he doesn't have any information on them, but they are still rough men. Not folks you would want to associate with."

"I don't plan to associate with them. What's the man's name, the one with his back to us?"

"Uh, they call him Deuce."

"That his first or last name?"

"That's the only name I know, and no one asks names around here."

"Why is that?" she asked.

"Two reasons: first, many men around here lie about their real name and, second, some might take offense at anyone being nosey."

"Thanks." Carly finished her beer and left

the saloon, thinking this had been another lesson learned.

She stood outside, leaning against a pole, until the game broke up and the men came out. Fortunately for Carly's plan, Deuce came out last.

"Hey, Deuce!" she called out.

The man hesitated a moment, then wheeled around with his hand on his gun.

"Don't do it, or I'll kill you where you stand," said Carly.

The light was not very good, which gave Carly an advantage. She knew who he was, but he did not know who was speaking, and it was hard for him to see her.

"Who're you and what do you want?" he demanded.

"I have a gun trained on you, so just raise your hands and walk toward me slowly."

The man named Deuce weighed his chances and quickly decided he did not like the odds. He raised his hands shoulder high and slowly walked toward her.

"Stop right there," Carly ordered.

Deuce obeyed, "What do you want with me?"

"I want you to carry a message for me. I watched you play cards, and you lost heavy."

"What's that to you?"

"I just thought you might need some

money."

"What'd I have to do for the money?"

"Like I said, deliver a message."

"To who?"

Carly pulled out her note and handed it to him. "Deliver this message to Elmer Trace."

"And what do I get?"

"How's ten dollars?" she asked.

"How about twenty?" he countered.

"I'll say fifteen and no more."

"Aw, all right. Let me see the money."

Carly handed the man the money. "Just make sure the message is delivered. If it isn't, I'll come after you."

Deuce turned away, stuffing the money and note into his pocket. He mounted his horse and rode out of town. Carly was not confident that Deuce would deliver her message, but she did not have many ideas right now. She watched Deuce ride out, and then headed for the hotel.

When she reached her room, she took a chair and moved it to the window so she had a view of the street. She sat down, watched, and waited, but she did not see anyone she was looking for. Even though it was dark, after supper she walked the streets, checking the saloon and other establishments. She still saw no sign of the men she wanted. She went back to her hotel room and went to bed. Soon she fell asleep, but nightmares haunted her sleep. She was jolted out of sleep when the big man with a beard tried to choke her. She got out of bed and sat in the chair by the window for a long time.

The man named Deuce reached the Lazy L Ranch, put up his horse, and headed for the bunkhouse. He had the note from the young man and he had his fifteen dollars, but he did not know much about the man who called himself Elmer Trace. Trace had only been at the Lazy L a few days, and the only man he associated with was the man who rode in with him. That man was hulking and had a very bad disposition. Deuce decided for his own sake that he'd best deliver the note to Trace anyway.

When he walked inside the bunkhouse, he found Trace seated at an old table playing cards with several other men. "Trace, I got a message for you."

"What kinda message?" Trace asked without looking up.

"Here, just read the note," said Deuce, handing it to him.

"Deal me out. I need a smoke anyway." Trace walked over to a corner, built a smoke, and read the message from Carly.

Mr. Trace, I know you are not using your real name but that is okay with me. You know me, and I have something for you. Meet me at the forks of the road heading for town at ten o'clock in the morning, and I will give you what you have coming.

A friend

Rod Ulrich was worried. Wes Stone would not be back for a couple of days. He did not have any friends, so who sent him the message?

"Deuce?"

Deuce was sitting on his bunk taking off his boots. "Yeah, what?"

"Come 'ere a minute."

Deuce looked over at Ulrich, then stood and walked over to him with one boot still on his foot. "You need something?"

"Where'd you get this here note?"

"Got it from a young man. He asked me to deliver it."

"What did he look like?"

Deuce gave a brief description of Carly and asked, "You know 'im?"

"No, don't think so, but thanks anyway."

Rod Ulrich tossed and turned most of the night, thinking about the note. Deuce's description sounded like that kid Carl at the card table. But he did not know a Carl, and Carl was just a kid anyway. Ulrich knew he was a wanted man, and he could be walking into a trap if he met this "friend." However, he could not see a lawman writing that note. Damn, he wished Stone were here. He knew Stone would know what to do.

After his sleepless night, Rod Ulrich had breakfast and saddled his horse. His curiosity had gotten the better of him. He was going to meet the man who sent him the note. He checked his six-gun and strapped it on his hip. As an afterthought, he went back to the bunkhouse and picked up his rifle. He was a realist, and he knew he was very good with the rifle, but with his pistol he was only average. Why he should even meet someone just because he had received a note from him, he didn't know. In spite of his reluctance, something was drawing him to the meeting. Thoughts of doom went through his mind as he mounted and left the ranch.

CHAPTER 21

Carly was not sure Rod Ulrich would get the note, and she was even less sure he would meet her on the road. But she had to try, so she had breakfast and rode out to the meeting place. She was extremely nervous, knowing that the best chance she would get to avenge her parents was only minutes away. She experienced a twinge of fear. Would she be able to do it?

While she waited, she wracked her brain, trying to remember everything Daggert had told her. Be aware of her surroundings, never face the sun, and listen to the person — not only what he says, but how he says it. She was on a small embankment and could see anyone coming or going, and she had her back to the sun. The rest she would just have to improvise when the time came. Suddenly, she heard hoofbeats.

She came out of the brush where she'd been waiting out of sight, and rode to intercept the man she knew as Rod Ulrich. He looked at her, but he did not seem to be concerned.

"Rein in, and get down, Rod," she ordered.

"Mister, you got me all wrong. My name is Elmer Trace, and I'm meeting someone in town." He recognized the kid from the card game.

"And I'm President Grant, and you're meeting me," she said sarcastically. "Now get down from that horse."

"You the one sent the message?"

"Yep, that's me."

"Look, mister, I don't have any money. You're making a mistake."

"No, mister. You're the one who made the mistake." She slipped the gun out of her holster and fired. The man's hat flew off his head and fell to the ground.

"The next bullet could be between your eyes. Now get down."

He quickly slipped out of the saddle and dropped the reins. The horse took a couple of steps and began munching on grass. Carly dismounted and faced him.

"You saw me lose my money at the card table."

"You denying you're Rod Ulrich?" she asked.

"R-Rod Ulrich? Never heard of him," he answered meekly.

Carly was getting tired of this game. "Reach for your gun. I'm going to give you a better chance than you gave my parents," she snapped.

"Look, mister, I'm no gunfighter. Besides, why would I want to draw against you? I don't even know you or your parents."

"You don't know me or my parents, huh? You knew us when you and your pals killed them and forced me into a bedroom at my house."

"You're mistaken . . ." His voice trailed off as terror filled his eyes.

"You're the one who made a mistake when you killed my parents and raped me."

"That wasn't me. That was . . ." He swallowed.

"I think you're beginning to remember. You were going to say?"

"Nothing. I mean . . ."

Carly fired a shot and hit the man in the leg. He howled with pain, "I swear to God, I didn't do nothin'."

Carly was enjoying herself for the first time in several days. "Tell me, Rod, how many women have you raped and killed?" She continued holding the gun in her right hand. With her left hand, she pulled off her hat and dropped it into the dust. "You still don't remember?"

He stared at her, and all at once his eyes widened. "You're a woman."

"Now you're getting the idea, and I'm glad, because before you die, I want you to remember everything. Did you enjoy yourself that night?"

"You're the woman in the farmhouse," he said, speaking so low that Carly could barely hear him.

"Speak louder, Rod. I can't hear you."

"Look, lady, Wes Stone was runnin' that show. I was jist there with him."

"So, he was running the show and he forced you to shoot my parents and rape me."

"I didn't shoot no one that night," he muttered, leaning down to hold his bleeding leg.

"Let's just get this over with. Draw your gun," Carly demanded.

"No, I won't."

Carly fired, and the bullet hit Ulrich in the left shoulder. "You're going to die anyway, so you might as well draw."

He managed to keep his balance as he dropped to his knees and pleaded, "I'm sorry. Please, just take me to town and turn me over to the law. I need a doctor."

"I'm the only law that you're ever going to see. Now get up, you coward."

"I can't, my leg . . ."

Carly took six steps and aimed her boot at his head, but he was too quick. He grabbed the back of her ankle, jerked her forward, and she fell on her bottom. Rod stood up, drawing his six-gun. She still held her gun, and she pulled the trigger at the same time he did. His bullet hit her in the left shoulder and hers hit him in the gut. He staggered backward and pulled the trigger again, but fortunately for her, the bullet only kicked up dirt near her right hip.

He dropped the gun, fell sideways, and began cursing, "You killed me, you bitch."

She rolled to the right, climbed to her feet, kicked his gun away from him, and was ready to shoot him again. Then she decided it was not necessary to shoot him, because he was not going to move very far. "You're not going to die yet, but how does it feel to know that you're going to die, real slow?" she asked.

"You gotta help me," he pleaded.

She heard gurgling sounds in his throat, and he began to spit up blood. "There's nothing I could do for you, even if I wanted too. You'll just have to die here alone." Carly walked over to pick up his gun, pitched it into a patch of weeds, put her hat back on her head, and walked to her horse. She needed to get away in case anyone happened by or heard the shots.

She tried to pull herself up on Boney but her injured left arm would not hold her weight. She was bleeding. Her left arm was drenched with blood. She put her left foot in the stirrup, and with some difficulty and a lot of pain, managed to pull herself up and into the saddle with her right arm. One down and two to go, she thought to herself, if she did not die first.

She remembered a stream a mile back toward town and headed in that direction. It was not far, but by the time she reached the stream, she was dizzy, light-headed, and ready to fall out of the saddle. As she dismounted, she fell on her side and blacked out.

She did not know how long she was out, but when she came to, her shoulder was throbbing, and she was so weak that it was difficult for her to move. In spite of the pain, she forced herself to crawl to the water. She cupped her right hand, dipped up some water, and then bathed her face and forehead. After a few minutes, she felt some better. She took a couple of swallows of water and then laid her head on the ground and closed her eyes.

After she rested a few moments, she decided she had to find out how bad her arm was. She had no experience with gunshot wounds, but she needed to learn. She tried to unbutton her shirt, but her fingers did not cooperate, so she jerked the shirt collar and the top three buttons went flying. She pulled the shirt off her shoulder and found that the bleeding had almost stopped and the blood had caked. She tried to find an exit hole for the bullet but couldn't. She decided the bullet must still be in her shoulder. She had to get it out but she did not know how. She pulled off the bloody shirt, dipped it in the water, and began cleaning herself up. She was careful not to rub the wound too hard and cause it to start bleeding again.

Her next chore was to get to her horse and get out her spare shirt before anyone came by and saw her. Then she almost smiled as she realized that it probably did not matter, because her breasts were covered and everyone already thought she was a man. She washed out the shirt, tore it into strips, bandaged her shoulder the best she could, and then slowly walked to her horse. She leaned against Boney while she riffled through her saddlebag to get her spare shirt.

She struggled to put the shirt on and struggled even more to mount. She gave Boney his head, and the animal headed for town.

CHAPTER 22

By the time Carly reached the outskirts of town, her shoulder was bleeding again, and was leaking through her new shirt. She had another shirt in her hotel room, but she did not want to have to explain why her shirt was bloody. She knew that when Rod Ulrich's body was found, the marshal would be asking questions. It would have been nice if she had been able to hide the body, but he was too big, and her injured shoulder would not have allowed her to drag him anyway. Then she decided she did not give a damn if they found out what she did, but only after she got even with the other two men.

She circled around, came up behind the livery stable, and dismounted. Fortunately, the owner was not there, so she led her horse inside to an empty stall and, with some difficulty, removed the saddle. She tried to swing it up on the half wall but could not manage. She just dropped it on the ground, found some grain and hay, and left it in the stall. She removed her shirt and wiped as much of the blood from her shoulder as she could, then washed the blood out of the shirt, using Boney's water bucket. She emptied the bucket behind the livery, and apologized to Boney for the empty bucket. She put the wet shirt on, and tried to act normal as she walked to the hotel, avoiding catching anyone's eye.

She opened the door to the hotel, walked directly to the counter, and asked for her key. The clerk got her key and handed it to her. He started to say something, but Carly quickly turned away, and walked upstairs to her room. When she got inside her room, she fell across the bed, tired and in pain. She told herself that she would get out of bed and clean herself up after she rested for a while.

Some time later, she woke in a cold sweat and burning with fever. She needed some water but when she tried to sit up, she fell to the floor. She tried desperately to get back up in the bed, but she was too weak. She pulled the covers and pillow from the bed, laid her head on the pillow, and passed out.

■ ■ ■ ■

Clay Daggert hoped Carly had stopped over in Bakers Crossing, but no such luck. He checked at the hotel, and then described the young woman in jeans to the marshal, but no one had seen her. He stayed overnight and left early for Rock Springs. He pushed himself and the horse, and by the time he reached town, he was tired, hungry, and saddle sore.

He stopped in front of the Springs Hotel, but down the street, the saloon caught his eye. He had not had a drink in a couple of days, and he needed one badly. He would stop at the saloon and have one drink. Then he would come back to the hotel and find out if Carly was staying there. He wearily dismounted, tied his horse at the hitching rail, and began slowly walking toward the saloon. He took several steps, then changed his mind. He would go to the hotel first. He needed to find Carly, even if she didn't want to see him.

He climbed the steps, walked inside, and approached the desk clerk.

"What can I do for you, sir?" asked the clerk.

"I need a room for a couple of days."

"Be glad to accommodate you, sir. Just sign the book, and I'll get your key for a nice quiet room in the back."

While he was signing the register, Daggert asked the clerk, "You have a young lady staying here?"

"No, sir, no women right now."

"Are there any other hotels in town?"

"This is the only one. Who're you looking for?"

"I'm looking for a young lady, about twenty or so, and very pretty. She goes by the name Carly."

The man scratched his head and stared back at Daggert. "Sorry, sir, I don't think we ever had anyone around here that fits your description, or who goes by that name."

"Much obliged," said Clay. He put some coins on the counter. "I'll be back for the key later." He left the hotel and again headed for the saloon, but saw the marshal's office across the street. He decided to visit the marshal. The drink would have to wait.

He hesitated in front of the marshal's office and read the sign, "Joe Shipman, Marshal, Rock Springs." Clay had heard of him, but had never met the man. He opened the door and stepped inside. The office was bare except for a large wooden desk, a file cabinet, and a potbellied stove. The first thing he noticed was the coffee pot boiling on the stove. A cup of coffee might hold off his urge for a beer.

He turned, and saw a man looking at him from behind a desk half covered with papers. "Yes, what can I do for you?" the marshal asked as he peered over his metal rimmed glasses.

"Marshal, I'm Clay Daggert. I'm looking for —"

"Trouble." The marshal finished Clay's sentence, as he took off his glasses, dropped them on the desk, and rose to his feet. "I know who you are, Daggert, and there will be no killing in my town."

"I'm not here to kill anyone."

"I've heard that before, and I've heard about you and your gun for years now. You can't deny it."

"Look, Marshal, I'm not denying that I'm Daggert, but I'm not here to kill anyone."

The marshal glared at Clay for a moment, "Then what are you doing here?"

"I'm looking for a young woman."

"Well, a lot of men are looking, but we don't have many unmarried young women here." He put emphasis on *unmarried.*

"I'm only looking for one, and she's a young woman who goes by the name of

Carly. She would have arrived in town in the last couple of days."

"Only a couple of strangers in the last few days, and one of them ended up dead, but no women."

"Really? What happened to the dead one?"

"Gut shot along with two other bullets, one in the shoulder and the other in the leg. It 'peared someone wanted him to suffer for a while before he died. Not your usual style, now is it?"

"You have a name for him?"

"I thought you were looking for a woman. You know something about him or have some reason for asking about the dead man?"

Daggert grinned at the marshal. "You're saying, or thinking, that I'm nosey, huh?"

"I'd say curious," replied the marshal as he reached for his coffee cup. He kept his eyes focused on Daggert.

"I have a hunch, but I don't want to share it just yet."

Shipman considered for a moment before responding. "I guess it's not a secret. The man called himself Elmer Trace."

"But for some reason, you don't think his name is Elmer Trace?"

"I believe his name might be Rod Ulrich and if so, he's an escaped convict from the

Kansas State Prison. I've wired the prison what I know, but I don't have an answer yet."

Daggert caught his breath and then let it out. "And you have no idea who killed him?"

"No, but I found a saddle in the livery stable with blood on it. We didn't find a horse near the body, so I surmise that whoever shot him either brought the horse back to town or brought the saddle back to town and stashed it in the livery stable. Someone beat you to him?"

"What did the dead man look like?"

"First, I'd like to hear about your hunch. How 'bout you share it now."

"Not now, but it would help if I knew what the dead man looked like."

Shipman considered. "I doubt you'd come straight to my office if you were here for a killin'. All right." The marshal described the man, then said, "He's down at the morgue. You can see for yourself. He won't be buried until tomorrow."

"I'll do that, and much obliged for your help, Marshal," said Daggert as he turned to leave.

"Daggert." The marshal walked close to Daggert, stared him straight in the eye, and said, "You do know something about this killing. Is that your hunch?"

"Of course not. Remember, I just rode into town."

"Well, for both our sakes, Daggert, I hope you're just riding through."

"Marshal, I have no intention of causing you any trouble." Clay opened the door and left the office.

He stood on the porch for a moment, building a smoke. He lit it, took a drag, and let the smoke leave his mouth. He was quite sure that he knew who Elmer Trace's killer was, but the question was, where was she now? Daggert was concerned about the blood on that saddle. He didn't buy that part of the marshal's theory. He had his own thoughts about the killer, and now he was sure that Carly was wounded and in trouble. He also believed that somehow she had managed to get back to town. Since she was not at the hotel, where would she be hiding? From the description the marshal gave, he was sure the marshal was right about the dead man's name being Rod Ulrich.

He flipped the match into the street and headed for the morgue. He wanted to be sure, before he spent a lot of time investigating the killing. He walked inside and looked around. A man came out from the back room. "What can I do for you, sir?" the man asked.

Clay looked him up and down. He was an older man, about sixty, slender, with a white beard. He wore a black suit that was too big for his frame. "Just wanted to look over a body that you have in here."

"You a friend or relative?" asked the undertaker.

"I'm thinking that I know him under a different name."

"Does the marshal know you want to look at him?"

"Sure. The marshal suggested I come by."

"All right, then. Come with me."

Daggert followed the undertaker to the back room and looked at the body. "Bullet holes?" he asked.

"There are three bullets in the corpse, one in the shoulder and one in the leg. Neither of those were fatal. The one that killed him was in the gut."

"The gut shot killed him?" asked Daggert with surprise.

"Actually, he bled to death from the shot. It was not fatal in itself, but someone left him out there to die. I'd say a revenge killing," surmised the undertaker.

"Thanks for your help."

"You know him? Is he who you thought

he was?" asked the undertaker.

Daggert shook his head, "No, I don't think so." He was now sure that the dead man was Rod Ulrich, but it would not help Carly if anyone knew he was in any way connected to the dead man or to Carly.

He left the morgue and headed for the saloon. As he reached the saloon door, he thought about the cup of coffee that he had forgotten to ask for at the marshal's office.

CHAPTER 23

Clay walked through the swinging doors of the saloon and let his gaze wander around the room. He did not expect to see anyone he knew, and he was right. He walked over to the bar and ordered a beer. When the bartender came back with the beer, he set it down on the bar and said, "You must be a stranger here in town. I've never seen you before."

"Yep, just came in today."

"Looking for a job?"

"No, just passing through."

"We don't get many strangers in Rock Springs. It's a bit out of the way."

"I don't suppose there were any women who came through in the last few days?"

"Mister, you must be kidding. The last woman came through over a month ago, and she was traveling with her husband. They stayed over and left the next day."

Clay was baffled. A woman as beautiful as

Carly Barton would not be missed in a town the size of Rock Springs. He wanted to order a bottle of whiskey and take it to his room, but he settled for another beer. When he finished the beer, he dropped some coins on the counter and headed for the hotel.

He picked up the key to his room and started for the stairs, then turned back to the desk clerk. "You sure you haven't seen the woman I described? Sometimes she wears jeans."

"Look, mister, uh . . ." He looked at the register and read the name. "Daggert, I've told you, no one came through here like the person you described. There're several women at the saloon. Why don't you just pick up one of them?"

"I'm not looking for any woman. I'm looking for a particular woman. Is there a boarding house or somewhere else to get a room?"

With an exasperated expression on his face, the clerk said, "No!" then turned the register around to Daggert. "Look for yourself."

At first, Clay thought about taking the clerk's word and going up to his room, but he was desperate to find Carly. He scanned the names in the register and saw none that he recognized. He was about to give up when he flipped the page back, and the last name at the bottom caught his eye: Carl Barton. He knew this could not be a co-incidence.

"Do you know Carl Barton?" asked Clay.

"Yes, of course, but he's not a woman," said the man, smirking.

"What does he look like? Never mind. I'll see for myself." Daggert headed for the stairs.

"Look, mister, you can't just bother people . . ."

Daggert ignored the clerk, bounded up the steps, and walked down the hall to the room of Carl Barton. He put his ear to the door and listened intently for a moment. There were no sounds coming from inside the room. He gently knocked on the door and waited. After a few moments, he knocked again, this time harder, but there still was no response. He slipped his six-gun from the holster and tried the knob on the door with his left hand. It turned and he pushed it open.

The room was dark, and the only light came from the window. He scanned the room quickly to be sure no one was hiding in the shadows. Then he took in the details and saw a figure lying on the floor beside the bed. He closed the door, holstered his gun, pulled out some matches, and fumbled for the lamp on the wall. By the lamplight he saw a young man on the floor. He took a couple of quick steps and knelt beside him. He raised the man's head and Clay saw, not a man, but a woman, and she was the woman he was looking for.

He checked her pulse. She was still alive. He put his hand on her sweaty forehead. She obviously was burning up with fever. Then he noticed her bloodstained shirt. He pulled out his knife and cut off the sleeve and the cloth around the wound. He pulled off the makeshift bandage she had managed to put on and saw the red, angry wound. She opened her eyes and moaned softly.

"Carly, it's me, Clay. Can you hear me?" She moaned again and tried to move. "Don't worry. I'll get you a doctor as soon as I can." He picked her up and laid her on the bed. He gathered the covers from the floor and covered her, and then took the shirtsleeve he had cut off, wet it, and laid it over her forehead.

"No, no," she muttered. "Don't tell anyone."

"Young lady, you have no choice. You'll die if I don't get you to the doctor."

"No. Please —"

He interrupted her. "It doesn't take many smarts to figure out that you killed a man.

Apparently, he shot you in the process. Is that about right?"

"Yes," she whispered, "but don't tell the marshal. I'm not through."

"I'll try to keep it a secret, but it will be hard. Now you just lie here quietly and I'll fetch the doctor for you."

She grabbed his arm. "Please don't leave."

He pulled away from her. "I'll be right back," he said as he left the room.

He ran down the stairs and stopped in front of the counter. "Where's the doctor's office?"

"Two blocks down and turn right. His office is upstairs. Why? Who's sick?"

"I'll let you know when I get back." Daggert hurried out of the hotel and ran down the street following the clerk's directions. He turned the corner on Fourth Street and saw the sign that said Leonard Groeb, MD. He took the steps two at a time and knocked on the door.

"Come on in. It's not locked," said a loud, gruff voice.

Clay pushed the door open and saw a man of about fifty sitting behind his desk. His hair was graying, and he wore spectacles.

"Running like that will kill you," said the man after listening to Clay gasping for breath.

"You the doctor?"

"If I'm not, I'm sitting in his chair."

"Yes, I guess that was a stupid question."

"Now that we got that settled, how can I help you?"

"Well, there's someone in the hotel that took a bullet in the shoulder. I'm afraid it's infected."

"Bullet wounds do have a tendency to become infected, if the bullet doesn't come out right quickly."

"Well, are you coming or not?"

"I'm a'coming. Did you talk to the marshal?" the doctor asked as he reached for his bag.

"No, not yet. No time."

"Okay, lead away. By the way, I didn't catch your name."

"Daggert, Clay Daggert."

As they hit the street the doctor asked, "Are you Clay Daggert, the gunfighter?"

"Let's just say I used to be the gunfighter. For the last few months, I was the town drunk," Clay responded as he tried to hurry the doctor along.

"That's not something a famous man like you would normally admit," the doctor replied with a chuckle. "Is this feller a friend of yours?"

Clay was still trying to figure out the best

answer by the time they reached the hotel. He did not have to answer, as Marshal Joe Shipman was waiting in the lobby.

"What the hell is going on?" Shipman asked.

"I don't know yet. I was just summoned by Mr. Daggert here," replied the doctor.

"Daggert, if you shot someone, I'll . . ."

"Hold your horses," said Daggert. "I didn't shoot anyone."

They reached Carly's room, and Clay asked the marshal to wait out in the hall for a few minutes.

"Now you wait just a minute —" sputtered the marshal.

The doctor interrupted him. "Joe, settle down. I'll let you know what's going on when I get inside and have a chance to examine him."

The marshal grumbled but did as he was asked.

When they got inside, Clay said, "Doc, I have to tell you something."

"Can't it wait?"

"No. Your patient here is a woman," he whispered.

"Hell you say. Who would wanna shoot a woman?" He did not wait for an answer as he felt her forehead, checked her pulse, looked at her wounded arm, and then pulled back the covers.

"He, or she, is pretty sick and is certainly bound up."

"She was pretending to be a man."

The doctor paused only a second to let that sink in, then pushed the covers off and said, "Hold this over her while I cut off the cloth she's bound up with so I can see if she took another bullet anywhere."

When that was finished, Clay took a chair in the corner and watched the doctor work. Carly seemed to be unresponsive most of the time, but did moan when the doctor probed, trying to find and remove the bullet.

"Bring me that washbowl," said the doctor.

Clay picked up the washbowl and held it until the bullet was out. Then the doctor seemed to take a long time cleaning and closing the wound. Clay sat back on the chair and waited. "Is she going to be all right?" he asked when the doctor started to pack his bag after bandaging the wound.

"Well, Daggert, I can't tell for sure, but I believe she'll make it. Only one bullet and it missed the bone. The wound seems to be pretty clean. It'll be a few days, and she's going to need a lot of care."

"I'll be glad to take care of her."

"I don't think so. She'll need a female to take care of her for a couple of days anyway. I have a young lady in mind, but she'll need to be paid."

"I'll pay her," Daggert said with a hint of relief.

"All right. Now that we got that settled, we need to talk to the marshal."

"I know. I can hear him out there. Let's go."

They walked out of the room to find the impatient and angry marshal. "Now, the two of you had better tell me straight up what the hell is going on," said Shipman.

"Joe, settle down. Your heart won't take much of that," said the doctor.

"Doc, my heart is fine. Just tell me who's in that room."

"She's not going anywhere, so come on downstairs, Marshal, and I'll explain everything," said Daggert. The marshal muttered under his breath but he followed the two men downstairs.

When they reached the lobby, Daggert asked the marshal to take a seat. "The young woman in the room is Carly Barton, and she took a bullet in her shoulder."

"Carly Barton? Who's she? Never heard of her. Wait, is she related to Carl Barton?"

"She's the same person. She was dressed

as a man," explained the doctor.

"Well, I'll be, I knew there was something strange about him . . . or her," said the marshal. "So how did she get shot?"

"I can't stand here all day and gab. I've got things to do," said the doctor gruffly. He turned quickly and started for the door. "Daggert, the woman I was talking about is named Jenny. I'll get her here as quick as I can," he said as he closed the door.

After the doctor left, Daggert suggested they go over to the marshal's office, and Shipman agreed. Daggert could not help but notice the desk clerk's disappointment.

When they reached the office, Shipman poured two cups of coffee and put one in front of Daggert and the other on his desk. "Now, tell me the whole story. From the beginning."

Over the next few minutes, Daggert told Carly's story: how convicts killed her parents, how he taught her to shoot, and how she left town to track down her parents' killers. When he was finished, Shipman rubbed his chin and looked up at Daggert, who was sitting on the edge of the desk. "Are you telling me that a young woman killed that convict we found some miles out of town?"

"Can't tell you for sure, because she wasn't able to talk, but that would be my guess. Now, since he was a convict, I'm sure she won't have any problems from the law."

"I reckon not. There's also a five hundred dollar reward on each of those men, dead or alive. But I'd have to talk to her for my report."

"Really? A five hundred dollar reward?" Daggert was pleasantly surprised.

"Yep, they killed a prison guard and wounded two more, and it's believed they killed a couple more people in their travels, not even including this young lady's parents."

"So she *will* be getting the reward, right?"

"I need to talk to her. After that, I'll wire the prison and let them know one of their prisoners is dead so they can send the money here. There's just one problem."

"What's that?" Clay asked with trepidation.

"As soon as she is well enough, I want her out of town. I'm trying to run an orderly town, and I don't want any gunslingers in town, men, or women."

"I'd guess your suggestion includes me then," Daggert said with relief and a smile.

"Nothing personal, but yes, that suggestion definitely includes you."

"No offense taken. By the way, there were three of these gents. Would you have any idea where the other two are hanging out?"

"I'd only seen this man a couple of times. Of course, you understand that since I'm the law, they would have tried to steer clear of me. However, I did see this gent with another man, and the two of them were working at the Lazy L Ranch."

"Much obliged, Marshal."

"Now Daggert, this is lawman work, so don't you go out there lookin' for that man," cautioned the marshal.

"Marshal, this is not my fight. I have no intention of doing anything with, or to, anyone."

"You just take care of that woman, and when she's well enough to ride, you get her out of this town, you understand?"

"I don't think I can control what that woman does."

"Why the hell not? She's just a woman."

"Yes, but she's one very stubborn woman, on a mission."

"What do you mean?"

"Let me tell you a story. I knew a man who owned a mule, and this mule was extremely stubborn. One day the man had a rope on the mule, and the mule was pulling him toward a cliff."

The marshal interrupted, "So the rope broke before they got to the cliff."

"Nope. The man was smart enough to finally let loose of the rope."

"And the stubborn mule stopped before it reached the cliff."

"Nope, the man let loose, the mule went off the cliff, and killed its foolish self."

"So the moral of the story is?"

"The moral of the story is that sometimes you have to let go of the rope and let the person do what they have to do. I haven't known the woman very long, but I do know that I cannot persuade her to stop what she's planning to do."

"Even with a rope?" asked the marshal with a chuckle.

"Marshal, there's no doubt she would pull me over the cliff with her, if I tried to stop her."

"Okay, but you do understand my problem and my terms?"

"Of course, Marshal. I understand, I'll do what I can, I can't give you any promises," replied Daggert as he left the office and headed back to the hotel.

CHAPTER 24

Clay returned to the hotel and asked if he could have the room next to Carly's. Fortunately, it was vacant, so he moved his things in. He washed his hands and face in the washbowl, then changed his clothes. He wanted a bath, but he would have to wait for that. He spent some time with Carly, even though she was sleeping. Sick rooms made him uneasy, so he was glad when the woman named Jenny showed up to take care of Carly.

He figured Jenny was about forty, nice looking, but a little plump. They agreed on her pay to nurse Carly, and then chatted, which woke Carly up. He introduced Jenny to Carly, but she was not happy about having anyone care for her. Jenny examined her and decided Carly needed a bath, even though Carly strongly objected.

Clay took his cue from their conversation and left the room. He headed for the saloon.

It was practically empty, and the bartender wanted to talk when he brought Clay his beer.

"I heard about that young man who was in here a couple nights ago and is really a woman. You know him — or is it her? That right?"

"Yes, I know her, and yes, she is a she."

"That sounds strange. Why do you reckon she'd do such a thing?"

"Don't know, and of course, it's not my business anyway."

The bartender looked at Clay as if his feelings were hurt, and then walked down to the other end of the bar.

Clay had not meant to upset the bartender, but Carly was the very topic he did not want to discuss. He finished his beer and left the saloon. His stomach was telling him it was time to eat, so he asked a man sitting on the porch for the best place to get a meal. From the looks of him, the man himself probably had not had a meal lately either.

"The best place is the hotel, but down the street is a café called Annie's. She makes the best stew and biscuits."

"Much obliged. Say, I don't usually like to eat alone. How about eating with me?"

"Mister, you don't know who you're talking to. I'm the town drunk. Nobody eats with me. Anyhow, they probably wouldn't serve me, even if I had money."

"Well then, how do you know how good the stew is at Annie's?"

"Sometimes Annie brings me a meal at the back door."

Clay contemplated the fellow and then decided. "Stand up," he said. With some difficulty, the man willingly stood to his feet. Clay looked him over. "Stay here for a minute. I'll be right back."

Daggert walked back to his hotel room, picked up one of his shirts, a bar of soap, and a towel, and walked back to where he had left the man. The drunk was sitting again, in the same spot.

"What's your name?" Clay asked.

"Luke," the man answered.

"Well, Luke, come with me." They walked over to the horse trough. "Get your shirt off, wash up, and we're going to Annie's."

"But mister, they won't let me in there."

"Don't worry. Just leave that to me. And call me Clay."

Reluctantly Luke stripped from the waist up and washed himself off. Clay handed him a towel and the clean shirt, and soon they were on their way to the café. Clay held the door for a reluctant Luke to enter the café, and directed him to a table in the corner.

"A stranger and a drunk. What a combination."

Clay looked over at the man who spoke. He was a burly fellow. Big — probably close to two hundred and fifty pounds. "And an ugly ape," said Clay as he sat down.

"Who the hell are you calling an ape?" the man bellowed.

"Mister, we just came in for a meal, so we would appreciate it if you keep your mouth closed, and let us eat in peace," said Clay.

"Neither of you are gonna eat here. I'll see to it," said the big man.

Luke reached over and pulled on Clay's arm. Clay turned to look at him. "Clay, that's Fallon, and he's beaten almost every man in town. Let's just leave. I'm not hungry anyhow."

Clay ignored Luke and looked back at Fallon. "You own this café?" he asked.

"No. I don't need to —"

Clay interrupted him. "Then you have no say about who eats here."

The man stood. Clay thought he was as big as a mountain with hands like the paws of a full-grown grizzly bear. Clay stood too. "If you got a gun, use it."

Fortunately, Fallon was over ten feet away.

Clay did not figure Fallon would rush him from that distance. The man pulled up short. "I'm not a gunfighter."

"Then you'd better learn how, before I put a bullet in you," snapped Clay.

"Damn you, you're not going to shoot me."

"Make one step and find out."

One of the men sitting with him at the table stood and whispered to Fallon, "I just remembered who he is."

"I don't give a damn who he is."

"You'd better give a damn. That's Clay Daggert. I seen him kill a man in Dodge City. With that gun he's faster than greased lightnin'."

The other man sitting at the table stood as he said, "I've heard a lot about Daggert, and he don't play. We're finished eatin'. Let's just get outta here."

Fallon glared at Clay, pulled some coins out of his pocket, and dropped them on the table. "This is not over, Daggert, or whoever you are," he snarled as he and his pals walked out.

"I'll be around any time you're ready," Clay said as he sat down.

A young woman who had come through the kitchen door heard the end of the exchange and came over to take their order.

"Well, Luke, you're all dressed up. You look great," she exclaimed.

"Why thank you, Hattie. I'd like for you to meet my friend, Clay Daggert."

She smiled at Clay. "Nice to meet you, Mr. Daggert."

"Same here," he said. "I guess you're not the Annie of Annie's."

"No, if Annie was here, she'd have sent Fallon packing with the shotgun she keeps under the counter," said Luke.

"Yes, she would. But I'm afraid of guns and I'm afraid of Mr. Fallon," said Hattie.

"I'd say you're pretty smart on both ends," replied Clay.

"What can I get you to eat?"

"I'll take beef stew with biscuits. I hear it's great," said Clay.

"Yes, it's very good. How about you, Luke?"

"Well, I . . ."

"He'll have the same, and put it on my tab," said Clay quickly. "And two coffees."

"Comin' right up," Hattie said and walked away.

"Thanks for buying my dinner. I don't get many opportunities to eat in a café. Of course, it's my fault. I'm drunk most of the time. The only reason I'm not drunk now is I don't have any money."

"Maybe you can do something for me sometime."

"Sure, I'd be glad to."

"Where do you get your money?"

"Mr. Boggs lets me work sometimes at the livery stable, er . . . when I'm able to, or sober."

"Let me ask you a question. Have you heard about the man who was killed a day or so ago?"

"Oh, sure. I know a lot. Even though I'm drunk most of the time. I remember when he rode into town. Left his horse in the livery stable, he did."

"Was he alone?"

"Oh. No. Two others rode with him."

"Could you describe them?"

"One of them was big, even bigger than Fallon. He had a beard and stuck his gun in his pants, no holster. The other one was not much more than a kid. He carried his gun in a holster, tied down like a gunfighter."

The waitress came up to them with coffee. "Your food will be coming out shortly," she said with a smile.

"Thank you, ma'am," said Clay. "Did you see any of them after they rode in?" he asked Luke.

"I was sleeping in the stable the next morning when the kid came in early, saddled his horse, and rode out alone. Never saw him again. The other one has been in town a couple of times."

The food came, and the two men ate their meal without speaking. Clay emptied his coffee cup, left some coins on the table, and then handed a couple of coins to Luke. "Thanks for your help."

"Any time. You just find me, if you need any more help."

"Much obliged," said Clay as he stood, waved at Hattie, and left the café. He took his horse to the livery stable, made sure he was cared for, and then spent some time getting the lay of the town before going back to the hotel. Carly was sleeping, so he went to his room, went to sleep, and did not wake up until the next morning.

CHAPTER 25

Morning broke quietly over the town. Daggert was in no hurry to get up. He figured that he had earned a few extra hours of sleep, and he had slept well. He awakened refreshed, got up to dress, and through his open hotel window, smelled bacon frying. He stopped by Carly's room before heading down for breakfast. She was awake and wanting to talk.

"Clay, when did you get here?"

He sat down in the chair beside her bed. "You don't remember? I got here yesterday. I helped you get in bed, then I fetched the doctor. You look much better now, how do you feel?"

"I'm feeling fine. I'm getting up as soon as I have breakfast. I've got a lot to do."

"Whoa now, missy. The doctor said three or four days of rest at least."

The door opened and Jenny came in with Carly's breakfast. "I'm sure you must be hungry. It's been awhile since you've had a bite," she said as she put the tray down on the washstand.

"I'm famished, thank you."

"I'll be back to check on you after I get my breakfast," said Jenny as she left the room.

Clay stood. "I'll let you eat, and I'll come by later."

"Clay, wait. I want to ask a favor."

"If it doesn't get me killed or put me in jail," he said with a grin.

"First, I want to thank you for yesterday, and then I want to apologize for the things I said to you at the flats."

"You are welcome for yesterday, and I've already forgotten about the flats. Now what kind of favor do you need?"

"I want you to ride out to the Lazy L Ranch and see if there is a man named Wes Stone there. I've described him to you before, but he may be using a different name."

"I'll do it, but you didn't take my advice, did you?"

"What do you mean?"

"The man you shot, who shot you."

"Well, he's dead. Isn't he?"

"You mean you don't know?" he asked.

"I left him to die. I assume he did. Now

what did you mean?"

"I mean the advice about your gut shooting a man. That's what you did, and he still got off a shot that could have killed you."

"Well, I'm not dead yet, and I was just careless, that's all. It won't happen again, and if it does, I'll just be dead. No one cares anyway."

Clay shook his head. "I guess I can't win. You're still as stubborn as ever. Eat your breakfast. I'll be back later."

After breakfast, Clay stopped at Marshal Shipman's office to get directions to the Lazy L Ranch.

"Daggert, I know you're one tough hombre, but I wouldn't suggest you ride into the Lazy L alone. There're some men out there who are as tough as, or tougher than, you are."

"You want to ride in with me?" asked Clay with a half grin.

"No. I stay away from there unless necessary. They tolerate me, but don't welcome me, and of course, it's out of my jurisdiction."

"Oh sure, jurisdiction. In my line of work, we don't worry about jurisdiction. Anyway, thanks for the advice, but can you give me the directions?"

"It's your funeral." The marshal gave Clay the directions and then said, "I'd suggest you ask for Neil Legget, the owner. Tell Neil I sent you, and he might not have you killed."

"Much obliged, Marshal."

"Think nothing of it. I'm not doing you any favors. Besides the sooner you do what you came for, the sooner you'll leave town. That would make me happy."

"Any one of 'em more dangerous than the others?"

"They're all dangerous, but pay close attention to a man named Slim. You'll recognize him since he normally wears a colorful vest, and he's tall, thin, and has a handlebar mustache. He also carries two fancy six-guns."

Clay nodded and left the office. He walked over to the livery stable, saddled his horse, and left town, heading for the Lazy L Ranch. A couple of miles west of town he reined in and read the sign, Lazy L Ranch, with an arrow pointing northwest. He turned his horse and headed for the ranch. He considered different ways he could approach the place. At first, he thought about sneaking in and surprising them, but if they caught him, they might hang him. He finally decided he would just ride in and take his chances. When he was in sight of the ranch, he reined in, surveyed the area, checked his gun, and slid it back into the holster.

He dug his heels into the side of his horse and moved forward at a trot. A few hundred feet before he reached the ranch house, they had to cross a wooden bridge. The noise caused several men to appear from the house and the bunkhouse.

Clay reined in his horse a few feet from the house so that he could see the five men who were visible. "What's your business, stranger?" asked the oldest and biggest of the men.

Clay looked directly at the man. "Looking for Neil Legget. Is he around?"

"Who wants to know?" asked the man.

"Clay Daggert."

"I've heard the name. What do you want with Mr. Legget?"

"That's my business."

The man glared at Clay for a moment and, without taking his eyes off him, said, "Burdette, get the boss."

The man called Burdette turned and headed inside the house. Clay would feel more comfortable if he was on the ground, but he had learned a long time ago that you did not step down on anyone's property unless invited. He rested his hand on his gun and waited. He glanced off to his right and saw the man who had to be Slim. He had a very nice and colorful vest on, just as the marshal said he would. Daggert had to be careful that he showed no weakness, because the men were all armed and ready to pounce if the boss gave the word.

A few moments later an older man with white hair and a mustache walked out on the porch. "What's up, Deek?" he asked the man who had been the spokesman for the group.

"A stranger here wants to see you. Says he's Clay Daggert."

For the first time, the man stared at Daggert. "State your business, then get out."

"That's not a very friendly welcome."

"We're careful who we welcome here. Lots of unsavory characters running around." That speech drew some cackles from the men, but they stopped abruptly when Legget raised his hand.

"I'm looking for one of those unsavory characters. Keep your hand off your gun, fancy vest, or your boss will be dead, real quick," snapped Clay.

Legget glared at the man. "Slim, don't be a damn fool. Now Daggert, what do you want here?"

"I'm looking for a man named Wes Stone.

He's a big, fat, ugly feller. You can't miss him."

"What do you want this Stone fellow for?" asked Legget.

"I have some personal business with him."

"Well, he's not here. Took his bedroll and lit out sudden like."

"Anyone know where he went?" asked Clay.

The men muttered to themselves and shook their heads.

"I guess that's your answer, Daggert," said Legget.

"Thanks for your help, friend," said Clay. As a precaution, he backed his horse until he reached the wooden bridge, then turned him around, and left without looking back.

He rode fast for a half mile or so, then pulled over behind a clump of trees. He dismounted, rolled a cigarette, and waited. He did not know for sure if anyone would follow him, but he didn't want to take any chances. After waiting for several minutes, he decided no one trailed him, so he mounted and rode. He reached town, had a drink at the saloon, and then had something to eat before he visited Carly. To his surprise, she was sitting up in a chair in front of the window.

"Did Jenny say you could get out of bed?"

he asked.

"I sent her home. I don't need anyone to take care of me."

"Well, now, that's sure different from the person I saw here just yesterday."

"I have to get going. Every day I sit here, the harder it will be for me to find them."

"Look, Carly, if you don't get well before you leave here, it may even take you longer."

"Did you go to the Lazy L?"

"Yes, ma'am. The man you're looking for lit out some time yesterday."

"Are you sure?"

"I don't believe they had a reason to lie."

"Did they have any idea where he might have gone?"

"No, and I don't either, so you can just take a little more time and heal before continuing your hunt. I did find out that the younger man, the one you called Kirby, left town the day after the three men rode in."

"I didn't think he was really friends with the other two. I knew from their talking that he wouldn't stay with the other two very long." She stood and almost fell before he caught her and helped her back to bed.

"You're too weak to be up. You stay right there in that bed. I'll go down and get you something to eat and we'll talk later."

"Okay, but I was just a little bit dizzy," she muttered as she stretched out on the bed.

Clay stopped at the hotel desk, asked the clerk to send a tray of food up to Carly's room, and then headed for the saloon. He was concentrating so hard that when he walked across the street, he stepped in front of a wagon. The driver jerked the reins to keep from hitting him, and then let out a string of curses. Clay ignored him and walked on. He was not sure what he was going to do, so he decided to get drunk. That was what he had done best lately anyway.

He spent several hours in the saloon, drinking and gambling. He had no luck with the cards, but the whiskey loved him. When he left, he was so drunk that he had trouble walking. He walked several feet before he stumbled and almost fell over Luke, the town drunk. It was dark, but there was enough light coming from the windows of the saloon to recognize him.

"Hey there, Luke," he slurred.

"Mr. Daggert, you want a pull from my drink?" asked Luke, holding up an almost empty whiskey bottle.

"No thanks, Luke. Had too much already."

"Me too," chuckled Luke. "Sit down and join me anyway."

"No. I better get back to the hotel."

"I remembered something."

"What did you 'member?" asked Clay.

"I remembered about the man I was telling you about. You know, the one who left and didn't come back. You know, left town the morning after he got here. You know, the kid," he said, trying to get Clay to understand his meandering sentences.

"You mean the man that was a friend of the man who was killed?"

"Yes, that one, the kid."

"What'd you 'member?"

"As I told you before, I was in the stable when he rode out, you know."

"Go ahead," encouraged Clay.

"Well, he asked Mr. Boggs — you know, the owner — how far it was to Logan."

"Logan," Clay mused, "don't know 'bout it."

"Outlaw town, 'bout a hundred miles northwest of here."

"No law there?"

"You got it," said Luke.

Clay was astonished at how well-spoken Luke was, even when he was drunk. On the other hand, was he really drunk or just acting drunk? He stared at him. "Luke, where you from?"

"I guess just about all over."

"Where were you before you came here?"

"Abilene."

"What'd you do in Abilene?"

"Have you ever read the New Testament?"

"Uh, yes. Some of it. What's that got to do with anythin'?"

"Have you read 'bout Luke, the apostle?"

"Yeah, a doctor, so what?"

"Well, like the apostle, I was a doctor."

Clay was bewildered. "I must be drunker than I thought. I thought you said you were a doctor."

"I don't know. Maybe you're sobering up, but you heard me correctly. My mother, back in Missouri, named me Luke and tol' me I was goin' to be a doctor."

"And so you are?"

"Correction, I was, at one time."

"What 'appened?"

"My mother died, then my wife died during childbirth, and I couldn't save either one. I started drinkin' to forget. You know, the first thing I knew, drink had taken control of my life. And I don't want to talk about it anymore," said Luke with finality. He started to stand up as if he were leaving.

"I'm not going to preach to you. I've been a drunk myself most the time for the last few months. I'm sorry 'bout you mother and your wife. And now I've got to go too."

"What's your hurry?"

"I've got to get some sleep, and tomorrow . . . I have a lot to do tomorrow."

"If you're riding to where I think you are, be very, very careful," Luke said as he waved his finger under Daggert's nose.

"No, not ridin' real soon."

Clay made his way to the hotel and staggered up the stairs. He stopped in front of Carly's room and put his ear to the door. He could not hear anything, so he decided she was asleep. He did not want to bother her so he went to his room, undressed, and lay down on the bed.

CHAPTER 26

Carly waited for Clay to bring up her food. She was disappointed when she heard a soft knock on the door. She was sure Clay would not have knocked softly, if he knocked at all. She called for whoever had knocked to enter, and the woman from the dining room walked in with a tray of food and some coffee.

"The desk clerk asked me to bring up some food, but he wasn't specific about what to bring, so I decided myself. I hope it's okay," she said.

"I'm sure it'll be fine," replied Carly, not trying to hide her disappointment.

"You look disappointed," said the woman as she pulled the washstand close to the bed and spread out the food.

"Oh, no. Everything's all right," lied Carly.

"You were thinking about the man who came after you and why he didn't bring the food?"

"What man?" Carly asked, trying to sound indignant.

"Clay Daggert. I saw him when he went to get the doctor for you. He seemed to be quite concerned for your well-being," the woman said with a knowing smile.

"He's just a friend."

"Are you sure? I'm not an expert, but I'd say it was more than friendship that I saw in his eyes."

Carly shook her head. "Oh, go on, so I can eat in peace."

"Yes, ma'am. I'll come back in a little while to collect the dishes." She opened the door, hesitated, turned, and winked at Carly, then closed the door and headed downstairs.

Carly sat up gingerly, putting her feet on the floor, and stared at the food for a moment. That woman didn't know what she was talking about. And Clay was around just for the money. Then, why was he here now? He already had the money, yet he did travel many miles to find Carly. If he was in love with her, that was his fault. She had not given him any encouragement. She just hired him to teach her how to shoot, and that was finished. She wasn't looking for a man. Even if she was, no man would want her, after what happened to her. The only thing she wanted to do now was find the other two men, kill them, and finish this business.

She finally decided to eat before her food got cold. Once she started, she decided she was not that hungry, picked at the food for a while, drank the coffee, and pushed it away from the bed. She lay back down and tried to sleep, but sleep did not come. There was a knock on the door and the woman came in to pick up the dishes. Before she left, the woman fluffed the pillow, and covered Carly with a blanket.

"You didn't eat much. Was the food okay? Did I not pick things you like?"

"The food was all right. I'm just not that hungry."

"Well, I'm sure you'll feel better when you sleep some more. I'll bring you a meal tray later. You need to eat to get your strength back. Now try to get some sleep."

"Thank you for bringing the food."

This time, she rolled over and went to sleep. A knock on the door woke her, and in walked the doctor. "Just checking to see how you're doing."

"I'm feeling much better," she told him.

He felt her forehead. "You still have a fever, and it needs to be gone before you can get up. I expect that will take another day or two."

"I guess I can wait a little while."

"I left you some more laudanum for pain, if you need it, and I'll come back by tomorrow."

"Thank you, but I don't think I'll need any laudanum."

"Just remember to stay in bed and rest," he reminded her as he left the room.

Carly napped, but she was getting tired of staying in bed. Later in the afternoon, there was a knock on the door. She was sure it would be Clay, so she pulled the blanket up before saying, "Come in."

She watched the door, and Marshal Joe Shipman walked in. "I spoke to the doc this morning, and he says you're doing pretty well. You feel well enough to answer some questions?"

"What kind of questions?"

"Questions for my report."

"Marshal, I really don't have anything to say to you."

Shipman picked up her gun belt from the chair back, slipped the gun from its holster, and said to her as he inspected the gun, "Nice gun you have here."

"Look, Marshal, I'm sure you didn't come here to inspect my gun, so just ask your questions."

"You know something, Carly?" he said, taking a deep breath and letting it out patiently, "I know who you are and I have a pretty good idea what you're doing, or plan to do." Carly did not say anything, but kept her gaze fixed on him. The marshal went on talking. "I figure that you have a derringer, or some short gun, under those covers. I'm also figuring you think I mean to arrest you, or do you some harm. If so, then all you have to do is pull the trigger and be on your way. Am I right?"

She only stared at him, her hand steady and poised under the sheet. She held a poker face that didn't reveal anything.

The marshal shook his head and smiled. "Yep, that's what I thought." In no particular hurry, he walked over to the window and parted the curtains slightly with his finger, keeping his back to Carly. "If you think you need to keep that gun cocked and pointed, that's okay by me, but just make sure it doesn't go off accidentally."

"And just how would it go off accidentally?" she asked.

"Well, you know. If you sneeze or your finger twitched."

"I assure you that I'll be careful. I don't shoot anything accidentally," she answered.

"And I can assure you, I have no intention of arresting you, or harming you in any way."

Beneath the sheet, Carly let the hammer down on the derringer and let it lie against the side of her thigh. "I've broken no laws, Marshal."

"I know," Shipman replied, catching the touch of sarcasm in her voice. "But I do know about the death of Rod Ulrich."

"What about him?"

"You killed him and, of course, you deserve the reward."

"Reward? I don't know about any reward. Anyhow, my reward is knowing he's dead."

"Think about it, and let me know." Shipman turned, headed for the door, then turned back, hesitated, and said, "Hope you feel better."

"Thanks." She relaxed, rolled over, and with no thought of the reward, fell asleep.

When Carly woke, the sun was shining through her window. She thought her fever was gone. She slipped out of bed, and painfully managed to get dressed. She splashed some water on her face and tried to brush her hair. She remembered Jenny bathing her, but she would love to take her own bath and wash her hair. She was still thinking about a bath when she heard a knock on the door and called out, "Come in." When she saw Clay in the doorway she said, annoyed, "I expected you to come by last night."

"Sorry, ma'am. I went to the saloon and it was too late when I got back. How are you feeling?"

"I'm feeling fine, and ready to ride."

"Uh, I spoke to the doc this morning. He says a couple more days."

"Aw, hell, what does he know?"

"Carly, I'm going to ride with you, but not until you are cleared by the doctor."

"No problem, I don't need you to ride with me anyway."

"I'm going to ignore your tone because you're upset and frustrated, but I'm not going, and neither are you, until the doc clears you. Now I'm going down and get you some breakfast. Maybe it'll help your sour disposition." Without another word, he left the room and closed the door.

She threw the brush at him, but it bounced off the closed door. She screamed and fell back on the bed. *Who does he think he is?*

CHAPTER 27

When Wes Stone heard that Rod Ulrich was dead, he went to the bunkhouse. All of the men were out, and he needed to be alone. He was deeply disturbed and had to think about what he should do. It was not about the death; he worried about how it happened, gunned down. Ulrich was never a close friend. In fact, most of the time Stone did not even like him. He was just someone he could count on when he needed a job done. If he were sure about how Ulrich died, he would not be concerned, but now . . .

First, he was afraid that someone from the prison had tracked them down. Then there were the bounty hunters who could have tracked them to Rock Springs. No, bounty hunters would not leave a body out there for someone else to claim. Maybe that damned, no-good Kirby Wilson had something to do with Ulrich's death. Kirby disliked Rod and him; maybe he came back from wherever he went and killed Rod. On the other hand, maybe he hired someone to do it. Now that was crazy thinking. Kirby was probably miles and miles away from Rock Springs. Stone had to get control of himself, and he needed to think.

He had never been alone. He had bossed his own outlaw gang, and even while he was in prison, he had men to do for him. Oh, sure, they were not really friends, but they were people who would do for him, even if he had to force them. Sure, there were people at the Lazy L Ranch, but they did not give a damn about him. Maybe Ulrich made an enemy here at the ranch. That did not make sense. No one wanted to cross Neil Legget. Any disagreements were settled at the ranch, not on the open road.

Stone was not sure where he was going, but he knew he had to get away from the Lazy L. Maybe he should go find Kirby. He picked up his meager belongings, put them in his saddlebags, and headed for the barn. He saddled his horse, led him up to the hitching post in front of the house, wrapped the reins around the post, walked up the steps onto the porch, and knocked on the door. He waited anxiously for a moment, then knocked again. A middle-aged woman finally opened the door, wiping her hands on her apron.

"What can I do for you?" she asked.

"Need to see the boss."

"I'll see if he'll talk to you." She closed the door and disappeared into the house.

Stone rolled a smoke, fired it up, and nervously paced across the porch. It seemed like a long time before the door opened and Legget stepped out.

"What's the problem, Stone?" he asked.

"Just want to draw my pay."

"You've only been here a few days. You haven't earned much."

"I understand, but I have to be riding out."

"Problems?" the rancher asked. "Something to do with your friend?"

"I'm not afraid of anyone, as long as I can see 'em, but I'm thinkin' I'm being tracked, like Ulrich was. If so, I'm not going to make it easy for 'em."

"We have plenty of men here. You'd be safe."

"My friend wasn't safe."

"I can't argue with that," said Legget, and he headed back into the house. He came back with some money and handed it to Stone. "Good luck, Stone." Then he added, "You know, about two hard days' ride northwest of here is a place called Logan. The law won't bother you much there."

"Much obliged," said the big outlaw. Stone took the money and rode out without looking back. He had heard rumors that Kirby Wilson headed for Logan a few days ago. If Kirby were in on Ulrich's death, he would deal with him. If not, Kirby might ride with him again.

He rode hard and covered many miles, but his horse was tiring fast. It was too early to make camp, but having to contend with Stone's weight and the lack of water, the horse had almost reached his limit. The horse plodded on, with Stone punishing the animal, trying to make it go faster. About thirty minutes later, the horse pulled up lame. Stone never took care of his animals, and did not care to learn how to cure their problems. When he needed a horse, he just took one, regardless of the consequences. He pulled the saddle off, stored it in the bushes, and took the canteen and rifle. He thought about just letting the horse go, but now he was mad. So he pulled out his pistol, shot the horse in the head, picked up the rifle and canteen, and without looking back to see if the horse was dead, started walking.

He walked and walked, and finally made

camp near a small stream. He sat on the bank and pulled off his boots. His feet were sore and bloody. He stuck them in the stream, and the cold water helped temporarily. Unfortunately, he had not packed any food, so he ate some jerky, drank some water, and went to sleep. He woke early, tired, hungry, and footsore. His first thought was to sit and wait for someone to come by. He then decided that it might be days, or even weeks, before anyone would ride by, because he was not exactly on the main road. He pulled his boots onto his sore and swollen feet and forced himself to walk.

After several hours of alternately walking, or limping, and resting, he came upon a farm in a valley, with a small house, a barn, and one outbuilding. He sat on a rock and watched the place. After some time, he decided there were only three people in the house, two adults and a boy about ten years old. What he was most interested in was a horse. He saw two grazing in a corral next to the barn. He decided he was going to get one of those horses, one way or another.

He headed down the hill toward the farm. The boy saw him coming first and he yelled out for his father. The man came forward and spoke to Stone. "Howdy stranger. You look somewhat put out."

"You're damn right. My horse gave out a couple days ago, and I've been walking for miles," Stone exaggerated.

"Boy, git your mother and tell her to fix this man somethin' to eat."

"Sure, Pa," the boy answered as he ran to the house.

"Come on over to the well and get some water. I'd guess you have a powerful thirst by now," said the man.

"You bet. My canteen went dry early this morning."

The two men walked over to the well, and the farmer drew a bucket of water. "Take a drink and then fill up your canteen. I'll go inside and see if your food is ready."

"Much obliged, mister," said Stone. He picked up the dipper and drank his fill before filling up his canteen. While he was alone, he checked the rounds in his rifle, then headed to the house. He stepped inside and saw a woman cooking at the stove. The farmer and the boy had just washed up and were waiting for him to come in and eat.

"Come on in and sit down, mister. I'll pour you some coffee," said the woman.

"Thanks, ma'am. Name's Ulrich," Stone said as he stood his rifle in the corner. He was sure none of these people would cause him any trouble, but he felt safer not using his real name.

"Mr. Ulrich, I'm Amy Ware. You met my husband, Cotton, and this here is our son, Jody. I'll bring you some food. Just sit down here." She set his coffee cup on the table and went back to the stove.

Wes Stone gulped the hot coffee, even though it scalded his throat, because he was so hungry. He was impatient for the woman to bring him the plate of food. The kid sat across the table staring at him, and the farmer tried to talk to him, but Stone only answered with yes and no.

Stone thought the food took forever, and as soon as it was in front of him, he dug in. He ate so fast, he was not sure if it tasted good or bad. Mrs. Ware brought him a piece of apple pie and refilled his coffee cup.

"That should keep you from starving," she said to the outlaw. Stone finished the pie, which was tasty, and the coffee, and stood up.

"How're you gonna get where you're a goin'?" asked Jody.

The outlaw scratched his beard, took a couple of steps, and picked up his rifle. "I'm going to borrow one of your Pa's horses."

"Wait just a minute, Ulrich. I need my horses for working the farm. I don't have any extra," Mr. Ware said anxiously.

Stone lifted his rifle and pointed it at the farmer. "I'm not asking you. I'm telling you."

The boy jumped up from the table. "Mister, you can't take my Pa's horses," he yelled.

"Shut up, boy, and sit down," snapped the outlaw.

"Jody, come over here with me," pleaded his mother.

Cotton Ware said, "Do as your mother says, Jody." The boy glared at the big man for a moment, then walked over and stood by his mother.

"Now, farmer, we can do this the easy way or the hard way," Stone said, brandishing the rifle.

"I guess I can't stop you," said Ware.

"Now that's better. Just stay inside till I'm gone. If you open the door, I'll blow your head off."

Cotton Ware dropped his head, but when Stone started for the door, he rushed the big outlaw, knocking him against the wall. Stone, temporarily taken off balance, managed to regain his balance, spun around, and easily blocked the farmer's right fist with his arm. He swung the rifle, hitting the farmer flush on the head. Ware crumpled, fell to the floor with blood streaming from the large gash on his forehead, and did not move. Stone turned to the woman, who was holding her son back as she repeated her husband's name over and over.

"You want him dead?" he asked, pointing the rifle at the man on the floor.

"No, no, please don't kill him," Mrs. Ware pleaded, tears flowing down her face.

"Then keep him and the boy in the house," Stone ordered. He walked over to the unconscious man and kicked him hard in the ribs. The man grunted but did not move. Stone turned and left the house.

When the door slammed, the farmer raised his head. "Jody, git my rifle."

"Sure, Pa. Right away."

"Cotton, no, please! He'll kill you if you go outside."

"Amy, we have to have those horses to work the farm," Ware replied as he staggered to his feet.

The boy came back with the rifle. "Here you go, Pa."

"Thanks, boy." Ware headed for the door. His wife grabbed his arm, but he pulled away, opened the door, and stepped out.

Stone had one of the horses out of the corral and was saddling it up when the farmer came out, aiming the rifle. "Git away from that horse."

Stone stepped behind the horse and pulled his pistol from his belt. The farmer fired his rifle, trying not to hit his horse, and the shot went wide. The outlaw stepped from behind the horse, fired, and the farmer went down.

"I told you, farmer, if you came out that door I was gonna kill you, and that's what I'm gonna do." Stone started toward the house.

He had only taken two steps when the woman came out, carrying a double-barrel shotgun. Before he could raise his pistol, a shot exploded not more than a foot in front of him, kicking up a lot of dust. He knew she still had another barrel, so he fired quickly, and then ran to the horse. He grabbed the reins, pulled the horse behind the barn, mounted without a saddle, and rode off. He knew he could go back to where he left his saddle and pick it up later. He was not in that big of a hurry to reach Logan.

CHAPTER 28

Owing to the pain in Carly's shoulder, the ride was taking longer than usual. The first day they left Rock Springs, they rode across the flatland, and made camp in a dry wash surrounded by waist-high prairie grass. It hadn't rained much, and the grass was brittle, and served as a warning if anybody approached the camp. Clay built a fire, put on a pot of coffee, and then took out some strips of jerky. He hung the strips over the low flames so that the meat would soften. Once the coffee was ready, they sat near the fire and ate their supper.

After they finished eating, Clay lay on his side facing Carly. He reached out, plucked a long stem of wild grass, and stuck it between his teeth.

"What if Stone is not riding to Logan like we thought?" she asked.

"We're not sure about Stone, but we are pretty sure Kirby is going that way. By the way, from what you told me, Kirby didn't kill your parents, and didn't attack you, so why not just forget about him?"

"No. He could have stopped them, or at least tried to stop them. As far as I'm concerned, he's as guilty as the others," she retorted sharply.

"So he should have risked his life for you and your parents?"

"Just tell me what you'd have done if you were in his shoes."

"I'd have interfered but —"

She interrupted him. "The right thing, by any standard, would be to stop them."

Clay knew that he was not going to win this argument, so he changed the subject. "All of this riding and shooting . . . what happens after it's all over? Can you settle down then?"

"I'll stop. I haven't developed a thirst for shooting and killing, if that's what you're asking."

"I just wish I had known you before," he said wistfully.

"You say that like it might have made a difference of some kind."

"It might've."

She shook her head. "I can tell you for a fact that it wouldn't."

"What do you mean?" he asked.

260

"Not you or anyone else could have kept me from trailing the men who did those things to my parents and me."

"I guess you're right. Once this is all over, what will you do? Where will you go?"

"I don't know. I haven't thought about it, and I'm not going to think about anything else until this is over. Either I kill them, or they kill me, and if they kill me, it won't matter anyway."

He hesitated before responding. "These are questions that need to be asked."

She turned on her side to face him. "Clay, either way, I have no life. Don't you understand?" Tears welled in her eyes.

He wanted desperately to reach out and touch her, or even take her in his arms, but he did not know how she would react. Instead, he pulled out the makings from his shirt pocket and built a smoke. He lay there for a few moments watching her, and then he stood and walked a few feet away to stare out over the darkening prairie.

He smoked his cigarette, peering into the darkness, and thought about her and her predicament. His heart ached for her. He wanted to console her, but thought better of it and walked over to check the horses. He finished his cigarette, and when he came back, she was in her blanket, pretending she was asleep. He put a couple of sticks on the fire to keep it burning, then lay down on his own blanket. He stared at Carly for several minutes, thinking how beautiful she was, and how difficult her life had been over the last several days. Her attitude was hard, but he believed that underneath, she was a wonderful woman. He finally rolled over and dropped off to sleep.

When he was not drunk, Clay was usually an early riser, but this morning he smelled coffee and bacon when he woke. He rose up on his elbow and looked at the campfire. Carly had her back to him. She was already dressed for riding and was cooking breakfast. He spoke, and his voice startled her. She jumped and wheeled around to face him.

"I thought you were going to sleep all day," she said coolly.

He rolled out from under his blanket, pulled on his boots, and stood. "It's just barely daylight."

She dished up some bacon and beans and handed him the plate. "We need to get on the trail. I want to be in Logan tonight."

"That's going to be a hard ride, especially on the horses. We may want to spend another night on the trail. How's your shoulder this morning?"

"It's a little stiff, but it won't keep me from riding, and I'm in a hurry to get there." She poured a cup of coffee and handed it to him. "Eat quickly."

He sat on the ground and began to eat. "Yes, ma'am. I'll be ready to ride soon, but if we wear out the horses, you may spend more than one night on the trail."

She poured another cup of coffee, sat down next to him, and sipped the hot black liquid. "So if we stop tonight, how long before we get to Logan?"

He set his plate on the ground and took a large swallow of coffee. "I'd say late afternoon tomorrow, if we're lucky. We can ride late today before camping."

She stared at him for a moment. "Clay."

He waited for her to continue, but she did not. "You started to say?"

She stood and tossed out the remainder of her coffee. "It was nothing. I'll wash the dishes and put out the fire. You saddle the horses, and we'll be ready to ride."

She could tell he was annoyed with her, but neither of them spoke. He stood, handed her the plate and cup, and walked to the horses. She watched him for a moment, wondering if she should say something, but she did not know what to say, so she said nothing and went about cleaning up.

The riding was better this day, and they covered many miles before stopping to water and rest the horses. Clay wanted to cook dinner, but Carly insisted they push on. They ate a biscuit and some jerky while they rode. He did not know how many miles they covered, but he decided it was time to camp for the night. "The horses have just about had it. We need to find a place to camp."

"We can cover a few more miles. We got an hour or more before dark."

"You see those dark clouds off to your right?"

She had been looking straight ahead, and she was not aware of the clouds until he mentioned them. "What do they mean? Are they coming our way?"

"They mean we're going to get wet, unless we find some shelter."

"How long do you figure?" she asked, sounding uneasy.

"I reckon about an hour or maybe a little less."

"So what're we going to do?"

"There's a hill and a tree line there, off in the distance. We're going to head in that direction, and hope we make it, and also hope we can find some shelter."

"Well, don't you think we should hurry?"

"Afraid not. If we push the horses too hard, we may not make it at all."

A half hour later they reached the tree line. The wind was picking up, and darkness was coming on fast. Carly hollered over the noise of the wind, "What're we looking for?"

"Some type of overhang, if we can find one. If we can't find one, and fast, we're going to get very wet." He felt a couple of raindrops. "Let's pick up the pace," he called to her.

The horses were as eager to push on as they were. The raindrops were coming faster and harder, and Clay had just about given up finding shelter when he saw what he was looking for. He spurred his horse and motioned for Carly to follow. What he saw was an almost dry creek bed, and high on the bank some outcropping rocks jutting out several feet. The outcrop would not help much with the wind, but it should keep them dry. The rain was coming harder when he hit the creek and headed up the bank. The sure-footed dun almost went down when part of the bank collapsed. Clay held on, the horse regained his footing, and they reached the rocks. He turned and saw

Carly's horse balk about climbing the bank. He started to turn back to help when suddenly there was a loud clap of thunder, followed by a streak of lightning that hit close by. Boney bolted forward, climbed the bank, almost unseating Carly, and slid to a halt beside Clay.

"You all right?" he asked.

"My shoulder hurts from when Boney bolted, but it'll be okay, if you'll help me down."

Clay dismounted and walked over to her. In the past, she had refused almost all help, but this time she just leaned over and allowed him to catch her. He held her in his arms, reluctant to release her, wanting to kiss her. She did not resist. Thunder roared again, and he set her down. "Move farther back and I'll bring in the horses. I need to check your shoulder to be sure it's not bleeding again."

She walked ahead. "It's dark in here."

"Yes, and it'll get darker. There are tracks in and out of here, as if someone camped. Maybe they left some firewood. We need a fire for supper and warmth, and to dry off."

"You hungry?" she asked.

"I'm so starved that my belly button is gnawing on my backbone," he answered with a smile.

"From that description, I'd say your belly is ungrateful."

The overhanging rock was high at the opening, but soon slanted down in the back. Clay was able to get the horses barely out of the weather. He pulled off the saddles and hobbled the horses so they would not wander away when the storm let up.

"I found some wood," hollered Carly.

"Good, maybe I won't have to spend a lot of time in the rain trying to gather up some."

"You'll have to go out to get some water for coffee, unless you're going to make me do it."

He handed her some matches. "See if you can get a fire going, I'll get the water." He took his slicker from his saddlebag, slipped it on, and carried the two canteens down to the creek. By the time he returned, she had the fire started, but he could see the effort had caused a considerable amount of pain.

"You sit down on that rock. Once I get the coffee started, I'll check your bandage."

"It'll be all right. I don't think it's bleeding."

"It don't matter. I'm going to check it anyway, so just relax." He got the coffee started, then put on some bacon and beans. While the food was heating, Carly unbuttoned her shirt and allowed him to examine her wound.

"Not bleeding, but when we get to Logan, a doctor needs to check it. I hope we get there tomorrow."

She awkwardly buttoned up her shirt, and Clay could tell she was still in pain. "A good hot cup of coffee and a good night's sleep should help you feel better."

"I hope so. I didn't sleep well last night. When is the food going to be ready?"

"I'll dish it out now. It should be warm enough," he replied as he poured the coffee and dished out two plates of bacon and beans.

They ate silently, listening to the rain, hearing an occasional thunderclap, and watching the bolts of lightning. When they were finished, he took out the blankets and spread them as close as possible to the fire. "It's turning colder," said Clay.

She lay down and slipped under the blanket. "Yes it is, and I don't know if this blanket will keep me warm."

"Well, if you get too cold, you can snuggle with me," he said with a chuckle.

"I know you'd love that! Good night!" She turned over on her good shoulder and waited for sleep to come.

Clay had fallen asleep, but sometime later, an extremely loud thunderclap woke him.

He rolled over and bumped up against Carly. He lifted his head and watched her sleeping with her back to him. Oh, how he would have loved to take her in his arms, but he knew what her reaction would be. He added a few sticks to the fire, and carefully lay back down, making sure he did not wake her. He watched her for a few moments through the flicker of light from the campfire, and then fell asleep.

Although he woke early, Carly was already up. The storm was over and she was returning from the stream with water. She had moved her blanket back to where it was early in the prior evening. He rolled out from under his blanket and thought about asking her how she had slept, but decided that might not be a good way to start the day.

"Fixing breakfast?" he asked.

Startled, she turned to look at him. "I'm not much of a cook over an open fire."

"I guess that means I have to do the cooking?"

"That would probably be best," she said as she sat down near the fire and waited.

He pulled on his boots, stood, and walked over to the fire. He rekindled the flame, added some water and fresh coffee to the pot, and set it over the fire. He sliced some bacon and dropped it in the pan to fry. With the bacon done, he poured a batter of flour and water, with a pinch of salt added, into the hot bacon grease. It made a pancake the size of the skillet and so thick, it failed to cook in the middle. He did not care. He took two plates, cut the pancake in two, put half on each plate, and then added the bacon on top. He handed Carly a plate, and then poured two cups of coffee.

He sat down next to her and ate with a wolfish hunger. He drained his coffee, stood, took the pot and warmed her cup, and then emptied the pot to the dregs into his cup.

"You must have been hungry," she said, watching him finish his coffee as she continued to eat.

"Yes, I was hungry, but now I'm ready to get on the road," he replied with a grin.

"I guess that means I need to get up and get going."

Clay nodded and headed off to saddle the horses. She picked up the dishes, carried them to the stream, washed them, and by the time she was finished, he had the horses ready. He packed the dishes, put out the fire, and poured some water over the ashes. "You need a boost up?"

"No, I think I can manage."

He stood watching her. He could tell she was still in pain from her shoulder. He would have been glad to help her, but she was just too damned stubborn. He watched until she managed to mount, then he swung up and led out, heading west.

CHAPTER 29

It was nearly dark when Clay and Carly rode into the small town of Logan. Logan was a one street town. There was one street for business, and a few side and back streets for residences. The business street consisted of two saloons, one hotel, a general store, a livery stable, a café, and a few other small businesses. The only people on the street were a handful of men congregating outside the Last Chance Saloon. A dog ran out from an alley and nipped at Clay's horse's heels. That was a mistake. The horse kicked out, the dog went sprawling, yelped a couple of times, and ran back into the alley.

Clay guided his horse to the hitching rail in front of the hotel and dismounted. He stretched, trying to get the kinks out of his legs and back, and then walked over to help Carly down, but she had already dismounted.

"You are one darn independent woman," he said.

"You're right. I'm going to take care of myself," she replied.

"All right, independent woman, let's see if we can get a room in this hotel."

"You mean two rooms."

"Uh, yes, that's what I meant," he assured her.

Carly remained skeptical.

They took down their saddlebags and walked into the hotel. The fat woman behind the desk offered them a room. Quickly Carly informed her, "We need two rooms."

The woman looked from Carly to Clay. "Sorry," she said with a smile, "I thought you two were married."

Clay smiled, but Carly did not. "How about the rooms?" she asked sourly.

The woman quickly pushed the register to her. "Just sign in." She turned and took out keys from the bin. "Rooms six and seven."

As Carly signed the book, she asked, "Do these rooms face the street?"

"Room six faces the street, seven faces the alley."

Carly looked at Clay. "All right, I'll take room six."

He did not protest. "I'll take the horses to

the livery stable and meet you across the street at the café," offered Clay.

"All right. I'll take our things to the rooms, freshen up a bit, and meet you there."

Clay turned and left the hotel. "That is one handsome man you have there," said the woman behind the desk with a smile.

Carly looked at the woman and frowned. "Thanks, for the rooms." She gingerly picked up the saddlebags without wincing, took the keys, and headed up the stairs.

The woman watched her go and shook her head. "I'd be glad to share his room," she muttered to herself.

Clay took care of the horses and walked over to the café. He seated himself at a table near the window and waited for Carly. A tall, thin woman came out of the kitchen, filled a cup with hot steaming coffee, and carried it to his table. "How about some stew? It's ready to eat."

"I'd really prefer a good steak."

"That can be arranged. It'll take a little longer."

"That's fine. I'm waiting for a young lady, so take as much time as you need. You might as well put on another steak for her."

"It seems that every man in town is waiting for a young lady," she said and walked back to the kitchen.

Carly walked in while Clay was drinking his coffee. She looked around and headed for his table. He stood and held her chair. "Well, now, aren't you the gentleman."

"Yes, and I ordered a steak for you too."

"Well, I'm sure it will taste better than what we had on the trail."

"Can't argue with that."

Clay looked around at the few customers in the café. "You see anyone you recognize?"

"No, I checked when I came in. Didn't recognize anyone."

Their food came and they ate without speaking. Carly finished her coffee and stood. "I'm going to the saloon to ask about the men."

"You can't go to a saloon. Women don't go to saloons except . . ." his voice trailed off.

"I know what you were going to say, but it don't matter. I'm going."

He knew there was no reasoning with her. "Then I'm going with you."

"I'm going to the hotel to change. You ready?"

Clay pulled out some change, left it on the table, and followed her out of the café.

Carly climbed the stairs, leaving Clay in the lobby. When she got to her room, she pulled out a shirt and a pair of men's pants she had purchased in Rock Springs. She decided since she had fooled everyone once, she might as well try it again. She wrapped her breasts the best she could with the binder, even though the pain in her shoulder hindered her. Pulling on the shirt and pants seemed easier after that. Walking over to the small mirror on the wall, she checked herself. *That's the best I can do,* she decided. She picked up her hat and left the room.

When she walked down the stairs, she saw Clay talking to the woman behind the desk. He looked at her and started to speak, but she put her finger to her lips and shook her head. Fortunately, the woman did not see her, and Carly headed toward the door.

"Uh, wait a minute, young man. You ain't registered in this hotel," the desk clerk said.

"Just visiting," replied Carly and walked out the door and onto the porch.

The woman started to yell at Carly, but Clay stopped her. "I'll check him out if you would like."

"Okay. I don't remember him."

He smiled, nodded his head, and left the hotel. "Hold up, Carly."

She paused on the top step and turned around. "My name is Carl."

"What are you doing?"

"Going to the saloon. What did you think?" she asked sarcastically.

"Well, damn it . . . you know that . . ."

She interrupted, "Yes, damn it, I know. No decent woman enters a saloon. Well, I'm not a decent woman anymore."

He shook his head and followed her down the street to the saloon.

CHAPTER 30

Carly stopped in front of the Last Chance Saloon and looked back at Clay. "Shall we go in?"

"Right behind you," Clay replied.

Carly led the way through the door, stopped to look around, and then proceeded to the bar. With all of the tables occupied, she pushed between two men, and ordered two beers. The man to the left glared at her, started to speak, noticed Daggert right behind her, and as his gaze dropped to his tied-down gun, he moved away, allowing Clay to step up to the bar. The bartender drew two beers and slid them down the bar to them. Carly pulled out some coins and dropped them on the bar.

As the bartender reached to take the coins, she put her hand on the money and said, "I'm looking for a friend of mine."

"Who you lookin' for?" asked the bartender.

"His name's Kirby Wilson. Would have come into town in the last week or so." She gave a description of the man she knew as Kirby Wilson.

"Don't recall anyone named Kirby, and the description doesn't fit anyone I know."

"Are you sure? He . . ." She felt a hand on her back.

"Move over kid. You're too young to drink anyway."

She slowly turned around and saw a big man about the size of Wes Stone. She looked him up and down, "Don't touch me," she snapped.

"And just what would you do if I did?"

Clay started to intervene but she put her hand on his arm. "I'll take care of this."

"So, kid, you got your big brother to take care of you," said the man.

"Back away mister, and don't call me kid."

"Why you little whippersnapper. I'll teach you some manners." The big man reached out and grabbed her left arm.

Pain cascaded through her, bringing back agony and bad memories, so that all she could see or feel was Wes Stone. With a lightning move, she drew her gun and smashed it upside the man's head. The man fell like a pole-axed steer, and she was right on top of him with the gun pointing at his head.

"You twitch, and I'll blow your head off!"

Clay quickly bent over and grabbed her right arm. "Let it go," he said softly.

"I'm going to kill the bastard right now."

"He's not who you're looking for. Let it go."

She shook her head, trying to regain her senses, and finally said, "Okay."

Clay pulled her to her feet. "Drink your beer."

"Some of you boys pick up Harley and carry him to the doctor. He's bleeding all over my floor," said the bartender. Two of the men helped up the man named Harley, and escorted him out of the door.

Carly took a deep breath and turned back to her beer. She held onto it hard because she felt her hand shaking.

"What were you thinking? Now you'll have to answer questions from the marshal," said Clay.

"Marshal Dodge is out of town, but he'll be back in a few days," said the bartender.

"Thanks. That's good news," said Clay.

The bartender walked down to the other end of the bar.

"Carly, uh Carl —"

She interrupted him. "Clay, I thought it

was Wes Stone. I keep seeing him every-where."

"That's what I figured. You sure pulled a lighting draw, one of the fastest I've ever seen."

"You're a good teacher," she replied. "Wasn't that what you wanted to hear?"

He ignored her sarcasm, "All right, look around. Do you recognize anyone?"

"No. Guess we might as well head out."

They finished their beers and left the saloon. As they stepped down on the street heading for the hotel, they heard someone in the alley. They both drew their guns, and quickly recognized the man from the bar Carly had jostled when they first arrived.

"Don't shoot. You lookin' for informa-tion?" the man slurred his words.

"Might be. Who're you?" asked Carly.

"Name's Tom Delaney. How much is the information worth?"

"It depends on the information, and how accurate it is," Carly replied.

"Well, you 'scribed a man I saw at the Easy Mark Saloon a couple o' nights ago. But his name was Brock."

"You sure it's the same man?" she asked.

"Welts 'round his neck. Not many like that."

"I have to agree," said Clay.

"Know where he is now?" Carly asked.

"I saw him a couple o' times at the Easy Mark. One time he was talkin' to a two-bit rancher named Shad Jacobs."

"Where's this Jacobs' ranch?" Carly asked.

"I know, I use' to work there till Jacobs fire' me. It's the Rockin' J. Now, how 'bout the money? I need a drink."

Carly pulled out some money. "Here's ten dollars. I'll give you another twenty tomorrow if you take me to the ranch."

"Uh, I don't know 'bout that," Delaney stammered.

"No more money unless you lead me to the ranch," she told him.

"Okay, sure, I'll lead you to it, but I don't wanna get shot. I ain't stayin'," he answered nervously.

"Why would you get shot?" asked Daggert.

"Well, it's a scraggly outfit that takes other ranchers' cows. I tol' him I wouldn't git hanged for changin' brands on cows, so he ordered me off his'n property. Tol' me he'd shoot me on sight, if I came 'round again."

"You get me close to the ranch, and I'll go in alone," Carly said.

"Okay. I can do that."

"I'll meet you at ten in the morning at the livery stable."

"Ten? Uh, I . . ."

"Delaney, don't let me down, or I'll be after you like stink on a skunk," she said harshly.

"Yes, sir, I'll be there," Delaney answered and headed back inside the saloon, money in hand.

As they walked back to the hotel, Clay asked, "You think you can trust this hombre?"

"Don't know, but I think he wants the money."

"All right, we'll be ready tomorrow morning," said Daggert.

"No. I'll be ready, you're not going."

"Look Carly, I don't think —"

She interrupted him. "I have to do this myself. I've already explained that."

He started to reply, then thought better of it. They reached the hotel and walked in. The woman at the counter asked if the young man wanted a room but Daggert explained that he was with him. The woman shook her head but did not say anything.

CHAPTER 31

For the first time in a while, Carly slept very well the entire night, without any nightmares. She had breakfast, and headed for the livery stable. She knew she was going to be early, but she wanted to avoid talking to Clay Daggert, because he would still want to go along with her to the ranch. She reached the livery and saw a slender man with red hair and a full red beard beginning to turn white. When he walked toward her, she also noticed that he had a severe limp.

"Mornin' lad," the man greeted her.

"Good morning."

"What can I do fur you?"

"I need my horse, and I'm waiting for someone."

"An' which be your horse?"

"The buckskin, fifth stall on the right."

"Sure, I'll get your horse. Who'd you be a waitin' fur?"

"Man named Tom Delaney."

The man scratched his head, looking puzzled, before he pointed toward the barn.

"What does that mean?" she asked.

"Delaney's sleepin' in one of the stalls. Doubt he'll be ridin' out with you any time soon."

"The hell you say," she said as she headed for the barn.

She found the stall and stared down at the sleeping drunk. "Get up, Delaney," she hollered.

There was no movement from Delaney, so she walked over and kicked him in the butt. He still did not move. She looked around, saw a bucket, took it to the water trough, and filled it.

She walked back over and dumped the whole bucket of water over the man's head. He came awake with a start, looked at Carly, and sputtered. "Damn, what you tryin' to do, drown me?"

"Yes," she said, "if you don't get up and get ready to ride, now."

Delaney grumbled to himself, then his head fell back on the straw. Carly was now angry. She pulled out her gun and fired two shots that landed about two feet from the man's head. Delaney rolled away and came to his feet.

"Now get yourself ready to ride," Carly said.

"But I . . . I haven't had breakfast," the frightened Delaney stammered.

"Get breakfast on your own time, not mine," she said tersely. "You have five minutes to get your horse ready to ride." She turned and left the livery stable, waiting for her horse. A small crowd had gathered after hearing the shots, but Carly ignored them. She did not see Clay in the crowd, and she was glad.

The two horses came out at the same time. Carly waited for Delaney to mount up, then she mounted, and waited for Delaney to lead out. They rode for a long time. The whole time Delaney slouched in the saddle and at times seemed to be asleep. Carly was concerned that Delaney was either taking her on a wild goose chase, or did not know where they were going. Finally, he reined in and turned his horse around, facing her.

"The ranch is nearby. Just ride beyon' this curve and take the road to the right. It'll take you 'bout fifteen minutes to reach the ranch."

"Mr. Delaney, if you cross me, you'd better ride far and fast, because your life won't be worth a plug nickel."

"It's the way I said. I wouldn't double-cross you. Can I have my money now?"

Carly pulled out the money and held it toward him. "Delaney, again, be warned if you cross me."

Tom Delaney pocketed the money, turned his horse, and headed back toward town, faster than they had come. Carly watched him until he was out of sight, and then headed on toward the Rocking J Ranch. Delaney was telling the truth, because within twenty minutes she came in sight of the Rocking J. She reined in and scanned the buildings. She could not see much from here, so she dismounted, led her horse up an embankment, and looked for a better vantage point. She saw a few men, but didn't recognize anyone so far away. She decided that her only option was to ride in. She was tired of waiting.

She mounted and headed for the ranch house. Before she reached the building, she heard the click of a gun and a voice. "Hold it right where you are, mister."

She reined in and looked toward the voice. "Keep your hands away from that gun," said the man.

"I'm looking for Mr. Jacobs," she said, raising her right hand over her shoulder.

"You know Mr. Jacobs?"

"Nope, just looking for a job," she said casually.

"Okay, just keep your hand away from that gun and we'll ride in," he said as he came out of hiding.

"Don't worry about the gun. I'm just interested in making some money. If you don't have a job, just say so, and I'll be riding out."

"We'll just let Mr. Jacobs take a look at you, 'n' he'll decide what to do. Now ride, slow 'n' easy."

When they reached the ranch house, the man holding the gun spoke to one of the men sitting on the porch. "Utah, this here man wants a job."

"You're kidding, Billy. That kid wouldn't last a day on this ranch," replied another one of the hands, snickering.

"Mister, if there wasn't a gun pointed at my back, I'd show you how long I'd last," snapped Carly.

"Shut up, Jones. I'm the foreman here," said Utah Kedrick.

The foreman stared at Carly. "Can you use that big hog leg you're carrying on your hip? How good are you?"

"I'm good enough. I'd be glad to show you, if you'd like."

He hesitated for a moment. "Git the boss."

The man nearest the door opened it and went inside the house.

After a few minutes, Shad Jacobs came out of the house, scowling and ranting. "What the hell is goin' on out here?"

"This young man wants a job," replied Utah.

Jacobs studied Carly before asking, "You know anything about cows?"

"Been 'round 'em all my life," lied Carly.

"That has ta have been a long time," said one of the men. His comment drew laughs from all the others, except Utah and Jacobs.

Carly was seething inside, but she remained calm. Jacobs looked at the men and the laughing stopped. "Can you use that gun?" he asked.

"I hit what I aim at."

"Pretty sure of yourself, aren't you?"

"Try me."

"What're you called, and where're you from?"

"Name's Barton, Carl Barton, and I been lots of places."

"Hell, boy, you're just a kid. Where could you've been after losing your diapers?" yelled the same man who'd heckled her before.

"Shut up, Jared. I'm running this show." Jacobs looked at Carly, and then looked off to his left. "You see that can 'bout twenty feet yonder?"

Carly's eyes followed where he was pointing. "I see it."

"Can you hit it?"

"I've got five dollars says he can't git it close," said Jared, and there was another bout of laughter.

Without a word, Carly drew and fired five shots at the can, hitting it all five times. Daggert had told her to keep the firing pin on an empty chamber, but before she rode in, she had added the sixth round. "Loudmouth, you owe me five dollars," she said, and pointed the gun at her mocker.

"I'm thinkin' your gun's 'mpty, and I'll plug you before you can reload," he answered cockily.

"If you're so sure my gun's empty, loudmouth, just go for your gun," Carly said.

The man looked at her and hesitated. He did not like what he saw in Carly's eyes. Jacobs saved him. "Jared, you lost your bet. Give the man the five dollars."

Jared's face flamed, and then went white, but before he could speak, Jacobs raised his voice, "Do what you're told." The man's expression turned to hate, but he wasted no time in coming up with the five dollars.

"What makes you think you could get a

job here?" asked Jacobs.

"I met a gent named Delaney in town."

"And just what did this gent say?"

"Oh, not much. Said he quit and you might need another man. I understand you have a man named Kirby Brock here."

"You a friend of Kirby's?"

"Just an acquaintance. Met him a few days ago."

"When you wanna go to work?" asked Jacobs.

"I can pick up my gear in town and start tomorrow."

"Okay, Barton. Meet me here at nine in the morning and we'll talk."

"Much obliged. By the way, where can I find Kirby?"

"Utah, where are the boys working now?" asked Jacobs.

"He and a couple of the boys are in Dry Wash Canyon. Not far from here."

"If you don't mind, I'll ride over and say hello."

"I don't mind. Utah, give 'im directions."

CHAPTER 32

Following the foreman's directions, Carly reached the canyon in less than half an hour. She reined in a few yards away from the fire, where three men had been branding cows, until they saw her coming. She immediately recognized the man holding the branding iron as Kirby Wilson.

The foreman had said they were branding strays, but these cows already had a brand. That would make sense from what Tom Delaney had told her. Anyway, that was not any of her business. Her concern now was that she had no idea how to brand a cow if they asked her to help. And more important, how could she get Kirby alone?

"State your business, mister," yelled one of the men with his hand on his gun.

"I'm a new hand. Just hired today," she answered as she rode closer to the men.

"You ready to start?"

"Not until tomorrow. Just wanted to look

around."

"Say, mister, you look familiar," said Kirby, "Have we met?"

"I've been around. We might have crossed paths sometime."

"Name's Kirby Brock," he said. "What's yours?"

"My name's Carl Barton," she answered, watching his eyes closely.

"I'm sure we've met somewhere. It'll come to me."

"I'm sure it will," she assured him. "Well, I'm on my way to town to pick up my gear. See you boys tomorrow." Carly turned her horse and rode away.

Carly and Daggert had just finished supper and walked out on the street when she spoke. "There's Kirby Wilson."

"Who, where?"

"There. The one just riding into town."

Before he could say anything, the rider reined up in front of them. "I couldn't wait till tomorrow, Barton. Been bothering me where I met you."

"Well, Kirby Wilson, I'm glad you decided to ride in. We have some business to discuss," said Carly.

"Wilson? My name is Kirby Brock."

"Wilson, you're a liar, a murderer, a

prison convict, and a coward. There may be other things I could call you, if I chose to think about it," Carly said.

"Look here, Barton. You can't talk to me like that —"

"Get down," she snapped as she moved a couple of steps away from Daggert and dropped her hand to her gun.

Kirby Wilson stepped down and away from his horse. "Just tell me who the hell you really are, before you challenge me."

She took off her hat, pitched it over to Daggert, and stepped closer. "Take a good look."

"I said you look familiar, but I don't know you."

"Think about a farmhouse a couple hundred miles from here. A wonderful couple that never hurt anyone in their lives, and now they're dead."

Wilson's head snapped forward and he stammered, "You're . . ." His voice trailed off.

"Now you remember," she said, no longer using her deep voice.

There was a crowd building, and someone leaned over to Daggert. "Do we need to get the marshal?"

"The marshal's out of town, and in this case, I don't think it would matter," Daggert replied.

"Look, Barton, or, uh, Miss, I didn't have anything to do with what happened at that farm," Kirby said.

"You should've done something, so that makes you a coward." Carly's voice was rising.

"Look, I'm not going to gun any woman," Kirby quietly answered back.

"You don't have a choice. You can defend yourself and die, or just die. Either way, it doesn't matter to me."

Wilson looked around at the crowd with concern. If he killed the woman, he would be in trouble. If he did not try to kill her, he knew she was going to kill him. "You can't hold me responsible for what those two men did."

"I'm holding all three of you responsible. One is already dead, and the other will soon follow. You might as well get ready, because either you kill me or I kill you."

He glanced over at Daggert. "Is he taking part?"

"No. It's just you and me."

Wilson, sensing he was out of options, dropped his hand to his gun. "Okay. I'm ready. Go ahead and draw."

"I'm waiting for you. I'm giving you a chance that you and your friends didn't give my parents."

"I told you, I didn't —"

"I don't want to hear any excuses. Just draw," she snarled.

And he did.

Their guns exploded at the same time. His bullet went wide, but Carly's bullet hit him in the chest, knocking him off his feet. He dropped his gun, and she moved to stand over him. He was coughing up blood and trying hard to breathe. He motioned with his hand and whispered for her to come closer. Carly dropped to one knee.

"You want to say something?" she asked.

"G-get S-Stone. His fault . . . everythin'."

"I'm going to kill him when I find him," she quietly answered.

"He was here. Said I gunned Ulrich. He killed . . ." The young gunman choked and spat out blood. "He killed a farmer comin' here."

"Where'd he go?"

"I . . . I don't know . . . s-south a . . ." his voice trailed off as he coughed and took his last breath.

"Move over. I'm a doctor, let me through," said an older, bespectacled man wearing a dark suit as he pushed through the crowd. He looked over at Carly and then examined Kirby Wilson.

The doctor looked up. "He's dead. A couple of you men carry him down to the morgue."

Carly stood up, walked over, and stood by Daggert. "I think he missed intentionally."

"It could be. It really doesn't matter. You got your revenge, and that's all you needed," said Daggert.

"I guess," she said in a doubtful voice.

"Don't start second-guessing now. That won't serve any good purpose."

Before she could answer, the doctor came over. "The marshal will be back tomorrow, and of course, there'll be an inquest. I'm sure he'll want both of you there."

"We'll be there," replied Daggert.

The doctor walked away and Carly said, "I need to get moving. Wilson said Stone rode out of town heading south. I don't want to lose any time."

"You can't leave until tomorrow."

"I know, but I don't like it."

"We also need to find out what towns are south of here and decide where he might be heading."

"All right. I think I'll turn in for tonight and get up early in the morning. Good night, Clay."

"Yeah, good night. I think I'll visit the saloon before turning in."

CHAPTER 33

Carly and Clay woke early for breakfast, even though Clay had stayed longer at the saloon than he had planned. They had to wait until after the marshal held the inquest before they could ride south, going after Wes Stone. After some questioning, the marshal had suggested the city of Tinslip as the likely destination for Stone, about forty miles due south.

They got out of Logan later than Carly would have liked, so the couple were caught out in the open when the sun set. It rained late in the night, and they both got drenched, but the sun came out early in the morning, and their clothing mostly dried before they reached Tinslip.

Tinslip had the typical main street with potholes, now filled with water from the recent rain, and wooden sidewalks, badly in need of repair. All the stores crowded the street and had false fronts, and the most significant buildings were the three saloons. Even though it was early in the day, the saloons were going full blast.

Clay and Carly stopped in at Barney's Beanery and ate their fill before heading to the marshal's office. Marshal Adam Stanky told them he had seen a man fitting Stone's description, but that he did not think he stayed in town. He suggested they talk to Buff Mitchell, the bartender at the Lucky Dog Saloon. That was where the man had spent most of his evening. Clay went to the saloon while Carly headed to the general store for supplies.

Clay entered the saloon, had a couple of drinks, and then spoke to the bartender. "Your name Buff?"

"That's me. Who would you be?"

"Clay Daggert."

"*The* Clay Daggert?"

"I don't know any other Clay Daggerts, so I guess I must be the same."

"So what can I do for you?"

"I understand there was a gent spent some time here last night. He's a huge ugly guy with a heavy beard and probably carrying a pistol in his belt. You remember him?"

"Sure, I remember him. He won some money at the poker game, nearly had a fight over one of the girls, and then bought a round for the house. He broke matches and left them on the floor. I had to clean up that mess. Does that sound like the man you're looking for?"

"Part of it does. You happen to know where he's staying?"

"According to his talk, and he talked a lot and loud, he was camped outside of town. I'm sure he's not staying in town. You need another drink?"

"I'd like another, but better not. I have some riding to do. Where would a man most likely camp outside of town?"

"I'd say about a mile southwest of here. There's a mesa with a creek, ideal for camping."

Clay finished his beer and set the glass on the bar. "Much obliged, Buff," he said as he paid and left the saloon.

He headed for the general store and found Carly waiting for him, and not very patiently. "I thought I'd have to go get you," she told him.

"Just having a beer and gathering information for you."

"I hope you got something I can use," she answered.

"I found out that Wes Stone was in the Lucky Dog Saloon last night, and that he camped out somewhere close to town."

"That camp could be anywhere," she said, somewhat disappointed.

"Maybe not. The bartender said the best place to camp would be about a mile southwest of here, so I suggest we head in that direction right away."

"All right, let's ride. The supplies are already in the saddlebags."

They mounted and rode out, hoping to find the campsite of Wes Stone. It did not take long for them to locate the creek. They followed it, keeping a careful lookout for Stone. After several minutes, they came to a deserted campsite. Clay dismounted, circled and examined the site, and then sifted through the ashes. "Could be him."

"I don't see anything. What tells you it could be him?" she asked doubtfully.

"Well, only one man, obviously a heavy man by the looks of the boot tracks in the sand."

"And that's all?"

"There is one more thing." He picked up several broken matches and showed them to her.

"Broken matches?"

"Yes. The bartender said Stone broke matches last night. Don't know why, maybe nervous energy."

"Great. You have any idea how long ago

he was here from the campfire?"

"I'd say not more than three hours ago."

"Well then, let's get riding."

"We've been riding hard. The horses need a blow and some water. We'll give them a few minutes. It's unlikely we can catch up with him today anyway."

"What happens if we lose the trail?" she asked with exasperation.

"We'll just have to take that chance. If we wear out the horses, for sure we won't catch up with him."

She reluctantly dismounted. Clay led the horses to the creek and let them drink their fill. Carly walked over to some shade and sat down, waiting for him to finish with the horses. After they drank, he tied the horses in the shade and built a smoke. He took out some jerky from the saddlebags, picked up one of the canteens, and walked over to where Carly was sitting.

"Might as well eat something while the horses are resting," he said as he handed her some of the jerky.

"I'd rather be riding," she said.

"Patience, young lady. Sometimes it just takes patience," he said with a smile.

She shook her head and frowned, but she took the jerky and the canteen. A few minutes later, they mounted and rode out.

They were not sure where Stone was going, so all they could do was continue riding, and hope he stopped for the night and let them catch up. They rode hard and fast, but always kept the horses in mind so they would not wear out. Finally the sun went down, and they knew they did not have much daylight left.

"We have to think about making camp," said Clay.

"Why can't we continue to ride? If he stops, we'll catch up with him."

"Or maybe he will catch us in the dark."

"Won't we see his campfire?"

"Not if he sets up a cold camp. He could hear us coming in and ambush us."

"So what would you suggest?" she asked.

"Ride as long as we can see, then camp. We continue on tomorrow, and hope we can catch up before dark."

Her sullen expression told Clay she did not like the idea, but she did not object. When it got too dark to see, they made camp. Clay took care of the horses, found some dry wood, and made a fire. Carly foraged through their saddlebags and brought out some food. She fixed some pan bread, thick chunks of bacon, along with potatoes cooked in the embers. She made coffee, strong and black.

She fixed two plates of food, carried them over to where he was sitting, and handed him a plate. As he watched, she removed her hat, brushed her hair with her fingers, and settled down beside him. When they finished, Clay stood and fetched two cups of coffee. They drank while staring out at the darkening prairie.

Clay finished his coffee, picked up her saddle, and set it down behind her. She leaned back against it to get more comfortable. "It's nice out here on the prairie," she mumbled softly.

He looked over at her and smiled. "It sure is nice and peaceful out here. It almost makes you think that no evil could come to this place."

"I'd like to think that evil only comes from the towns built on the prairie, but I know that's not true."

"Thankfully, your ordeal will soon be over," Clay said as he took her hand and squeezed it.

"Will it ever be really over?" she asked quietly.

"Yes. You can close that chapter and move on to starting a new life." Clay caressed her hand.

She did not object, so he moved closer and kissed her on the lips. A light, meaningless kiss at first, but then he was surprised when she added more pressure to the kiss. He gently raised his right hand, put it behind her head, and kissed her deeply. After a short while, he could feel her resisting, so he promptly let her go, and she straightened up.

"I . . . didn't mean to do that . . ." she stammered, not looking at him. "Not exactly like that anyway."

"Well, if you're waiting for me to apologize, that won't happen. We are two lonely people, out by ourselves, and I happen to be in love with you," he said matter of factly.

"Clay, you don't know me well enough to be in love with me, and I don't love you. I'm never going to fall in love with you or any other man. I can't." After a pause she asked, "Have you ever been in love?"

"Well, maybe —"

Carly interrupted him. "You've been in love with your work, from what I understand, and maybe that's what makes you so good."

"You may be right about my past, but I know how I feel about you now, Carly. A man can't deny that to either himself or to the woman he falls in love with."

"Clay, stop, please," Carly implored him. "You know this won't work."

She stood up, walked several feet away from him, and stood staring out into the darkness. He watched her, wanting to get up and go to her, but he knew that would probably make her angrier, so he just sat there, waiting.

She came back, sat down beside him, and tucked her feet under her. "What was she like, Clay?"

"She who?" he asked, startled.

"You know who. Julie. Mrs. Woodley told me about her."

"Uh, well . . . You're changing the subject again." He decided to answer her question, since it seemed important to her. "I didn't know her all that well, but she was pretty, smart, delicate — like she needed someone to take care of her. In some ways, I think she was kinda like you."

"Except for me needing someone to take care of me. I take care of myself."

"I think, in spite of your demeanor, you're a normal woman. I also think you would like to have someone take care of you. Maybe not right now, but in the future."

"You're wrong, I don't need any man. Anyway, do you think of Julie often?"

"Uh . . . sometimes, other times it gets blurry. You know, the times I forget about her is when I'm with you."

"Clay, please . . ."

He stood up. "It's time to turn in. I'll check on the horses. You get your stuff ready for the night."

She shook her head in frustration and watched him move away from the campfire and head toward the horses. She spread out her blankets, took off her gun belt and her boots, and slipped under the cover. When he came back to the campfire, he looked down at her. She was either asleep, or pretending to be; he could not tell which. He continued to look down at her. Was he really in love with Carly, or did he just feel sorry for her?

Finally, he walked over to his bedroll, took off his boots and his gun belt, and pulled the blanket over him. He was not expecting trouble, but as usual, he kept his six-gun in reach.

They woke early, had breakfast, and headed out without much conversation. Clay looked at Carly quite often. Each time she was looking straight ahead, with a very determined expression on her face. He wondered if her behavior had anything to do with their conversation last night, or if she was concentrating on finding Wes Stone.

Clay was confused about Carly, but he was not the only confused one. Carly was confused, too. Clay said he was in love with her. She said she was not in love with him, but was that true? Over the last couple of weeks, she had tried to concentrate on only one thing, and that was to avenge her parents' death. However, Clay seemed to be around almost all the time and helped her in so many ways. Sure, she paid him fifty dollars, but from what she could tell, fifty dollars was just a pittance for the jobs that Clay Daggert, the gunfighter, could command. They both knew the fifty-dollar job was over days ago. Yes, he had been a drunk when she met him, and he still drank a lot, but he had changed considerably since they met. Did last night's conversation reveal the real reason he had changed?

Clay interrupted her thoughts. "I smell smoke."

Carly looked around and sniffed the air. "I don't smell anything."

"Be as quiet as you can, and keep your eyes peeled," he said.

"Do you think it's Stone and he hasn't broke camp yet?"

"Could be, or it could be someone else." Clay pulled his horse off the trail and rode up an embankment. He reined in just before he reached the top and dismounted.

Carly followed and walked beside him as

they looked over the edge. "I see a camp down there, but I don't see anyone in it," she said nervously.

"We may have spooked him. He might be waiting to ambush whoever rides in. We'll stay out of sight, ride around that camp, and wait for him up ahead, as he comes by," Clay told her.

"I'll just ride in and face whoever is there."

"Don't be a fool. If it's Wes Stone, he's a murderer, rapist, escaped convict, and probably many other things. You think he's just going to let you ride in?"

"Well . . ." Her voice trailed off.

"Believe me, this is the best way. Come on, let's mount up."

Carly reluctantly followed. "How far should we ride?"

"Only a couple of miles, then we'll find a place for an ambush."

"I don't like the word *ambush,*" she said.

"Call it what you want, but we're going to wait for him, then you can do whatever you like. I still suggest you shoot from afar."

"No, I'm not going to do that."

"All right, suit yourself. Let's get ahead of the man and wait for him to ride by. Meanwhile, you can decide what you want to do."

They mounted and took a wide path around the campsite before returning to the road. They continued riding until they reached a bluff, hid their horses, and watched the road. They took a drink from their canteens and Clay built and smoked a cigarette. Time went by and still no sign of any riders.

"Maybe he rode by before we reached this spot," she suggested. "Maybe it was an old camp."

"Maybe, but I don't think so. Let's wait a few more minutes, and if nothing happens we'll ride on."

Carly was nervous as she walked back and forth. She looked at Clay, who seemed to be calm. Of course, she thought, he had been doing this for a long time. At least he did not try to calm her; she did not want to be calm. She just wanted this to be over, the job, and the nightmare. Then what would she do? That was, assuming she was still alive after meeting Stone. She shook her head and tried to get her mind back on Stone, but instead she thought about last night and her conversation with Clay. Was a future with him even possible? No, she had to concentrate on the now, and Stone. Nothing else.

"Carly, one rider coming in the distance," Clay said as he held out his field glasses to her.

She took the glasses and searched for the rider. Finally, she found him in her view. "That man is Wes Stone," she said as she handed the glasses back to Clay.

"I'll be glad to stay with you, Carly, and back you up," he said, his eyes pleading with her.

"No thanks, Clay. You ride on up the trail. If I don't survive, you can do whatever you want. If I survive, I'll meet you somewhere up ahead."

He stared at her for a few moments, then turned and headed for his horse. Now he knew what agony felt like.

"Clay," she said. "Wait." She walked over to him, took his hand, reached up, pulled his head down towards her, kissed him on his cheek, and then quickly stepped back. He started to say something, but unsure of his emotions, decided talking was not a good idea right now, so he mounted, and rode on ahead.

CHAPTER 34

Carly watched Clay ride away, then took her rifle from the scabbard and walked back to where she could see the trail. It took her a minute to get Wes Stone in her sights. She was an expert shooter with a rifle, and she knew she would not miss him at this range. She dropped the gun to her side and waited. She remembered Clay Daggert's early advice about using the rifle rather than her pistol, and he'd reminded her of it again today. He assured her that it would be easier and safer for her to ambush the men she was after rather than meet them face to face. She had managed to kill the other two men face to face, but for some reason she was reluctant to face Wes Stone, the one she hated the most. She had to make a decision fast, because soon he would reach the spot where she was hiding.

She put the rifle to her shoulder again, aimed it, tried to pull the trigger, but she could not do it. After a moment, she walked back to her horse and slipped the rifle into the scabbard. She checked her six-gun, walked over to the road, and waited, making sure her back was to the sun. She tried to remember all the other things Clay taught her, but her mind was not functioning. When Stone was about forty feet away, she stepped out on the road and faced him.

"That's far enough, Wes Stone," she shouted.

Stone was startled, but quickly recovered. "What do you want, boy, and how'd you know my name?"

"At least you're not denying your name, like the others did," she said without answering his question.

"Why should I, and why are you calling me out?" asked Stone, beginning to appear a bit nervous.

Carly touched her hand to her gun. "I'm sure you don't recognize me, but I'm not a boy, and I'm here to kill you."

He stared at her closely. "You do look familiar, but no, I don't recognize you. Why do you want to kill me? What'd I do to you?"

"I'm not surprised you don't recognize me, so I'm going to help you out. My name is Carly Barton, and I'm here to kill you. I'm sure you don't recognize my name either, but you murdered my parents and you, along with your fellow convict, raped me. Now, get down off that horse."

"Uh, hell yes, I remember you and the farmhouse. Never thought a woman had enough guts for revenge."

"Now you're getting the message. I told you that night I was going to kill you."

Stone stepped down from the saddle and shooed his horse away. "Well now, missy, I guess this is your chance to get even. I know ole Rod is dead. Now, I'm thinking you had something to do with that."

"An astute observation," she said. "I killed ole Rod, and Kirby Wilson too."

"Well, I don't give a damn about Wilson, but ole Rod, he wasn't much, but he was my friend. I guess I need to revenge ole Rod, huh. You ready?"

"You're lying through your teeth. You don't give a damn about anyone except yourself. I'm ready, and you're not the one going to get revenge."

"You're tryin' to get an edge and rattle me. Well, it won't work. I've killed people without blinking an eye," he said with a snicker.

"I know all about you, and I don't give a damn about you or your reputation. You're a back shooter, killer of men who don't even

314

carry guns, and a murderer of helpless women. Did I leave anything out?"

"I can't argue with any of that. Anything else we need to talk about?" he asked.

"You killed my mother and father, and had your fun with me that night. I'll never forget that. Now it's my turn to have fun. Yes, I killed both men. Ole Rod, as you call him, he didn't die easy. He begged and pleaded for his life. How about you? You ready to die? Are you going to beg and plead?" She might have been staring a hole through the big man.

"Hell, missy, you don't even sound mad about it, and you're not going to get any happier. You're never going to get a chance to tell anyone or brag, because I'm going to kill you. Sure, I admit it. I killed your father. I didn't kill your mother. Rod had the pleasure of doing that."

"I'm past mad, Stone," she said coldly. "I've learned to deal with it, and all I want to do now is get it over with. I've suffered, and now it's your turn. Only you'll suffer for only a short while, until you die, and that won't be long."

Stone chuckled under his breath and moved closer to her. "I don't know how you managed to kill 'em, but I can tell you I won't die that easy. I'm tellin' you, I won't die at all."

Carly slowly pushed the side of her coat behind her holster. "We'll just have to see."

"You're a woman, and women always have remorse. You must have some remorse for your killings," he said with a laugh.

Carly remained silent.

"You fool woman. I guess you're not gonna turn tail and run."

"Not a chance." She remembered Clay's instruction: watch what they do, not just what they say.

"Well then, I reckon killin' you is the best thing I can do for you. Now, I enjoyed that night. You're some woman. I bragged 'bout you to all o' my friends."

"Stone, you've never had a friend in your life," Carly said evenly.

"Oh, yeah, I do, and now I git to tell them I killed you."

Carly knew he was trying to get her mad, which might cause her to do something stupid. She kept quiet, watched him, and waited for a sign. She knew that somehow he would try to trick her, so she had to be on guard.

He lifted his left hand and scratched his forehead in an attempt to distract her. "I was going to give you a break but . . ." His voice trailed off, and then he grabbed for his gun with his right hand.

Carly was ready and her gun exploded, hitting the big man in the gut before he could get his gun out of his belt. He rocked backward from the impact of the bullet, staggered, but stayed on his feet. He pulled his gun to get off a shot, but her second bullet slammed into his chest, making him drop his gun and knocking him off his feet. Stone groaned, struggled, rose up onto his elbow, his left hand clutching his bleeding stomach. The fingers of his right hand were less than an inch from his pistol where he had dropped it in the dirt, but he could not reach it.

"I reckon . . . that does it for me," he said in a strained voice. He managed to shake his head slowly. "I didn't really hurt you, and nobody's pa or ma is worth this."

Carly pointed her pistol at Stone's forehead, cocked it, and held it steady. "You took something from me that you had no right to, and my parents were worth more than you and your stinkin' hide."

"You did what you came to do . . . just let me die in peace," he moaned.

"Yes, you are going to die, but not in peace," she said softly. "You haven't suffered nearly enough."

She aimed the gun, fired, and the bullet

tore into the fleshy part of his thigh. He howled with pain. "You bitch! Just kill me and git it over with," he pleaded.

"Now I believe you're begging. You didn't listen when I begged."

"I'll not beg." He replied through gritted teeth, trying not to groan in pain.

She cocked the gun, aimed, and let the hammer fall. The bullet hit him in the gut and he screamed louder. "Please, yes, I'm begging you."

She moved closer to him. He looked up at her. If he thought he could move, he would have backed up, even scrambled, to get away from those eyes of hatred. "You don't leave me nothin', do you?" he whispered.

"You bastard, you didn't bring anything worthwhile with you."

Wes Stone stared up at her, no longer trying to hide his pain, moaning and groaning, holding his gut. For a moment, she felt sorry for him. That moment quickly passed. She decided now was the time to end his life, and her long ordeal. She aimed the pistol at the man's forehead and pulled the trigger. She knew he was dead and did not even look at him. She walked over to Stone's horse, took the saddle and bridle off, and slapped the animal on the rump.

She mounted her horse and headed on

down the road. She had only ridden about a quarter of a mile when Clay Daggert came out from the bushes and guided his horse alongside hers.

"I see you're still in one piece. How about Stone?" he asked with a smile.

"Looks can be deceiving," she replied, a tear running down her cheek. "I just left the bastard for the buzzards."

"I know you didn't want any help from me, but I wanted to be here with you, even though it is finished."

"He's dead," Carly blurted out, "but it's not finished."

"I figured he was dead. How about you? Are you . . ." His words trailed off as he waited for some assurance or an explanation.

"I didn't get shot," Carly said, finishing his sentence for him.

"That's not exactly what I meant."

"I know what you meant, but I can't tell you. I know it's over, but it will never be finished. I can't feel any satisfaction yet." She gave Clay a weak smile.

"You may never get the satisfaction you are looking for, but how about letting me help you? I'll do whatever I can to help you ease your soul."

"Clay, I owe you so much, but I don't

know that I can ever pay you back. The few dollars I paid you was not nearly enough." Carly's eyes glistened with tears.

"Carly, I don't want your money. Sure, I took it up front, but I didn't know you then. My interest now is in you, not the money."

"But Clay, I don't think I can give you anything in return."

"Look, you know I've just been a drifter, gunman, drunk, and whatever you can think of, but I'd like to stay with you for a while. If you decide you want me to leave later, just say the word, and I'll go."

"Clay, you have your own problems. I know what caused your drinking, but what I don't know is if you can resolve your problems before you try to take mine on."

"And just how do you know about the cause of my drinking?"

"Mrs. Woodley and I had a long talk about how Julie died."

"Damn. She promised she wouldn't say anything about that. I guess it was my fault for telling her, but whiskey makes a person say things and tell things that should never be said."

"Please don't blame her. I sorta twisted her arm. Besides, if you help me with my problems, I might be able to help you forget yours."

"I've given that a lot of thought lately, and I think I can get past my problems."

She reined in her horse and he did likewise. "I don't know what I'm going to do today or tomorrow or next month, and I'd be glad for you to ride along with me, but only if you can fix your own problems," Carly told him.

"If you mean my drinking problems, they're behind me."

"If that's true, we might be able to make it work."

"Any idea where you want to go?"

"You know I have the farm. I don't know if I'll ever go back to it. But I do owe my parents a decent burial with a headstone. Brandy, my mare, is in the stable at Darby. I know these things may be far in the future, because I really don't want to talk about them, or even think about them right now."

"Okay, so let's just ride. Whenever you are ready to talk, you tell me what you need and what I can do to help you."

She peered at him, allowing her thoughts to stray. In her mind, she and Clay Daggert were riding up to her father's farm, and Clay was going to ask her father for her hand in marriage. She quickly brought her mind back to reality. That was certainly not going to happen. She realized Clay was staring at her, waiting for an answer. By his stare, he must be thinking she was going to turn down his offer.

She dropped her head, thinking about her life and Clay, then reached down, unbuckled her gun belt, and pitched it to him. "The first thing you can do for me is get rid of this. Then let's ride."

ABOUT THE AUTHOR

David Osborne was born and raised in Appalachia. He taught high school for many years and retired as a high school principal. He also spent twenty-six years in the military, including active and reserve time. He lived in Arizona and Colorado, and travels extensively in the west. He has a lifelong interest in the Old West and its history. Because of this interest, he became a writer. His works include short stories and novels about his childhood in the Appalachian region, and several western novels. Osborne currently resides with his wife, Pat, in Savannah, Georgia. Send him an email at dosborne5@comcast.net or see him on Facebook.com/david.osborne.311.